W9-ASL-504

Jubilee Journey

Other books by Carolyn Meyer

GIDEON'S PEOPLE

DRUMMERS OF JERICHO

RIO GRANDE STORIES

WHITE LILACS

WHERE THE BROKEN HEART STILL BEATS
The Story of Cynthia Ann Parker

A VOICE FROM JAPAN
An Outsider Looks In

VOICES OF NORTHERN IRELAND
Growing Up in a Troubled Land

VOICES OF SOUTH AFRICA
Growing Up in a Troubled Land

CAROLYN MEYER

Jubilee Journey

GULLIVER BOOKS
HARCOURT BRACE & COMPANY
San Diego New York London

Library of Congress Cataloging-in-Publication Data
Meyer, Carolyn.
Jubilee journey/by Carolyn Meyer.
p. cm.
"Gulliver Books."
Summary: Emily Rose has always felt comfortable growing up in Connecticut with her African American mother and her "French American" father, but when they spend some time with her great-grandmother in Texas, Emily learns about her black heritage and uncovers some new and exciting parts of her own identity.
ISBN 0-15-201377-6 ISBN 0-15-201591-4 (pb)
[1. Interracial marriage—Fiction. 2. Afro-Americans—Texas—Fiction. 3. Great-grandmothers—Fiction. 4. Identity—Fiction.]
I. Title.
PZ7.M5685Ju 1997
[Fic]—dc21 96-44563

Text set in Goudy
Designed by Camilla Filancia
Printed in the United States of America
G F E D C B C D E F G (pb)

for ERIN *and* JOSEPH

THE FAMILIES

Mother Rose's Family
(Rose Lee Jefferson Mobley)

Jim Williams, *her grandfather*

Lila Williams, *her grandmother*

Charles Jefferson, *her father*

Elvira Jefferson, *her mother*

John, *her brother*

Henry, *her brother*

Lora Lee, *her sister*

Nancy Lee, *her sister*

Rhonda, *Nancy Lee's granddaughter*

Susannah Jones Prince, *her aunt*

Horace Prince, *Susannah's husband*

Reuben, *Susannah's son*

James, *Susannah's son*

Tillie, *her aunt*

Cora, *Tillie's daughter*

Freedom Gibbons, *Cora's son*

EDMUND MOBLEY (NED), *her husband*

JOHN HENRY, *her son*

CHARLES (CHARLEY), *her son*

EMILY, *her daughter*

JULIAN PRATT, *Emily's husband*

DELILAH, *Julian's second wife*

BENJAMIN, *Emily's son*

SUSAN PRATT CHARTIER, *Emily's daughter*

GILBERT CHARTIER, *Susan's husband*

STEVEN, *Susan's son*

ROBERT, *Susan's son*

EMILY ROSE, *Susan's daughter*

CORNELIUS OVERTON'S FAMILY

GUS ALEXANDER, *his uncle*

ELLA, *his cousin*

LUCILLE OVERTON, *his mother*

MILDRED, *his wife*

ROSAMOND, *his son*

MARCUS, *Rosamond's son*

AURELIA, *Marcus's wife*

PAULINE WOODROW, *Rosamond's daughter*

BRANDY, *Pauline's daughter*

LATRISHA, *Brandy's sister*

TA LULA, *Brandy's cousin*

LU'RAE, *Brandy's aunt*

CATHERINE JANE BELL PLUNKETT'S FAMILY

EUNICE BELL, *her mother*

TOM BELL, *her father*

EDWARD, *her brother*

WILBUR PLUNKETT, *her husband*

PHOEBE PLUNKETT KINGSLEY, *her daughter*

PETE KINGSLEY, *Phoebe's husband*

TOM PLUNKETT, *her son*

DR. HAROLD PLUNKETT, *Tom's son*

MARISSA, *Harold's daughter*

Jubilee Journey

ONE

Only Daughter

April 7, Easter

Dear Emily Rose,

I am writing to you, the only daughter of the only daughter of my only daughter, Emily, to invite you to be my special guest at the Freedomtown Juneteenth Diamond Jubilee, sponsored by the African American churches of Dillon, Texas, on Wednesday, the 19th of June, 1996.

Although you and I have never met and I have not seen your mother since she was a child, it would please me very much to have you and your family present for this great occasion. You are welcome to stay with me and James.

Lovingly,
Your Great-Grandmother,
Rose Lee Jefferson Mobley

THE LETTER, addressed to me, was in the mailbox when the van dropped Robby and me off at our house after school. I ripped it open and read it while my brother checked out the junk mail.

"Look," I said. "Read this."

He read it. "What's Juneteenth?"

"I have no idea."

"She's my great-grandmother, too, isn't she?" Robby asked.

"Well, of course she is!"

"Then how come the letter's just to you?"

"Because I'm the only daughter of the only daughter of her only daughter, and that makes me special."

"Huh," Robby snorted. He's the baby of the family and used to being the special one. Steven, the oldest, already feels special. He's handsome and suave and all the girls chase him. Dad says I suffer from middle-child syndrome and that I *enjoy* suffering. This only-daughter thing was certainly something different.

"Let's go show it to Mom," I said.

We ran three blocks to my mother's restaurant, Café au Lait. My father came up with the name, which is French for coffee with milk, in honor of us kids. It refers to the mixture of Mom's black genes and Dad's white ones, although my older brother Steven turned out mostly coffee and Robby mostly milk; I'm the only one who's really half-and-half—right in the middle again.

Mom was busy prepping for dinner, but when we raced in she took a break to read the letter. "My God," she said. "Mother Rose." She looked away, pressing her fingers over her lips, as though she was squeezing back tears.

"Mom," I asked carefully, "What's Juneteenth?"

"It's something they do in Texas, an African American celebration." She gave me a shaky smile. "I should remember what they're celebrating, but I honestly can't."

"I don't know anybody who's got a great-grandmother," Robby said. "She must be ancient."

My mother sat down at an empty table and read the letter again. "I think my grandmother's eighty-seven," Mom said, "or eighty-eight. But just look at her handwriting!" It flowed clear and strong across the page, and in the corner by her signature Rose Lee Jefferson Mobley had drawn a bunch of flowers. "Mother Rose is a remarkable person." There was a catch in her voice from those squeezed-back tears. "A treasure, really."

"Why do you call her Mother Rose if she's your grandmother?"

"Everybody calls her that. They were calling her that thirty years ago when my momma died. I remember at the funeral, when everybody else was wailing and half crazy with grief, Mother Rose stayed as calm and peaceful as though sorrow was the most natural thing in the world. 'Death comes to us all,' she said—she was holding Benjie and me in her arms and rocking us like babies—'and it is not for us to question *when*.' I was only seven, too stunned to know anything but misery, but I'll never forget that. Her strength brought everybody through."

Mom had told us some of the story. I knew that she was just a little kid in Texas when her momma was killed in a car accident, and then her daddy went away to Chicago and left Mom and her little brother with their grandma, Mother Rose. One day her father came back and announced that he'd married a woman with five children and they had another one on the way. He packed up Mom and my uncle Benjamin and took them up to Chicago, and Mom never got back to Texas after that. Then Mom married Dad, Gilbert Chartier, who is white and of French descent, and they decided that Connecticut might be a good place to raise a biracial family. That was the outline of the story, but I could never get her to fill in the details about her childhood. "Some other time," she always said whenever I asked questions.

Once I asked Dad why Mom always seemed to shut down when I asked her about growing up. "Because it hurts her, Emmy," he said. After that I quit asking, but I still wondered about all the blank spaces in her story.

Every year we got a Christmas card with a little note from Mother Rose, and every year Mom wrote back and sometimes sent pictures of us. We'd even talked about going to visit her, but somehow we never did. Now this invitation had arrived, addressed to *me*.

"Mom, can we go?" Robby asked the question I was afraid to, because Mom seemed so upset. "The letter says she wants all of us to come."

"I don't know, Robby," Mom answered in a trembly voice. "Let's see what your father thinks about it." Then she firmed up, all businesslike. "We've got a couple of months to figure it out. Now scoot, kids. I'm behind on the desserts."

Mom had opened the café as a coffee and dessert bar when Robby started kindergarten. Then she expanded into the old house next door to the coffee bar, turning it into a real French restaurant. My dad helped her with the menu. She even started calling herself Chef Suzanne, instead of Susan. People come from miles around for her French cooking.

We all help out. Robby folds the cloth napkins, and I set the tables for dinner and check the salt and pepper and sugar bowls. Dad grows fresh herbs and sometimes bakes unusual bread. A few months ago when Steven turned sixteen, Mom began training him as a maître d'. He dresses up in a white pleated shirt with a black bow tie on Friday and Saturday evenings, the big nights. He doesn't mind, because the tips are great and he's saving to buy a car. When it isn't too busy, we all eat at the "family table" near the kitchen, and my mother comes out in her white jacket and sits with us. On busy nights, though, we sometimes have to wait until the last customers leave before we can have our family meal. On Sundays the restaurant is closed. We eat at home and Dad cooks, making our favorite things. My choice is usually melted cheese sandwiches, and Dad's are the best.

Dad had a late meeting the day the letter arrived, and I had to wait until we were eating dinner at Café au Lait to show him the invitation. I still wasn't exactly sure what I thought about the idea myself. I already had some plans for what I was going to do in June, after school was out. My best friend, Alicia, had invited me to go with her and her family to visit historic sites around Boston, because her parents are fascinated by American history. Also, I've just turned thirteen and am finally old enough to be a junior curator at the Northdale Nature Center where my dad teaches every summer and where a skunk named Rosebud is my special project. On the other hand, a trip to Texas sounded exciting, and I really wanted to meet Mother Rose.

It was a slow night—the customers were mostly regulars from the neighborhood. That night's special was chicken in red-wine sauce. Robby was picking out the mushrooms and tiny white onions and passing them to Steven, who will eat anything from greasy fast food to escargots—even *after* he found out that escargots are snails. Mom had sat down with us with her cup of coffee and Dad was sopping up the wine sauce with a piece of bread when I decided the time was right and showed him the letter from Mother Rose.

" 'Only daughter of the only daughter of my only daughter,' " Dad read out loud and grinned at me. "That makes you pretty special, Emmy. It sounds like something out of the Bible: seventh son of the seventh son." He passed the letter to Steven, who didn't have a clue what was going on, and looked at Mom. "What do you think, Suze?"

My mother, who is normally a very calm person, burst into tears. My brothers and I stared at her. I've hardly ever seen her cry—I'm the one who gets blubbery over practically nothing. "Adolescence," Mom always says, "can be a very *damp* time." Now, seeing her, I started to cry myself.

Dad slid to the other side of the table, put his arm around her, and stroked her hair. "Sorry," she snuffled. "It's just that all of a sudden I'm so homesick!" She pulled out a tissue and blew her nose.

"I never heard of Juneteenth," Steven murmured, as if he was afraid Mom might start in again. "What *is* it, anyway?"

"Something black Texans do," Mom said in a husky voice. "It's historical, like the Fourth of July." She seemed calm again, and my own tears evaporated without anybody noticing.

"It must be a pretty big deal," Dad said, "for Mother Rose to send this invitation. I think it's a wonderful chance for your mom to visit her relatives in Texas and for you kids to check out your roots on that side of the family. It would be an important history lesson for all of you, too." He cocked an eyebrow at me. "At least as important as the Battle of Bunker Hill."

I couldn't see how something I'd never heard of could be that important, but this wasn't the time to say so. I didn't know then just how wrong I was.

Dad kept his arm around Mom, and he was holding her hand. "Susie, it's up to you, of course, but I think all of you should go down to Texas for this Juneteenth Jubilee. We can close the café for a couple of weeks. It will give me a chance to get some work done, painting and so on."

Dad has a reputation for starting lots of projects around our old house and not finishing them, and I thought Mom might be worried about that, but she didn't even blink. "We could take the bus down," Mom said, and I realized that she was seriously thinking about going. I hugged myself to hold in a shiver of excitement.

"The *bus*?" Steven protested. "Why can't we fly? Or drive?" he added, which I expected, because he had gotten his license only a few months earlier.

"We can't afford to fly, Steven," Mom said. "Besides, a bus trip would be fun."

"An interesting experience," Dad said, "as well as educational. See your country close up."

Steven looked at me and rolled his eyes. Only Robby, who is ten, seemed to like the idea of the bus.

"Emmy," Mom said, "since the invitation was sent to you, why don't you write and tell Mother

Rose that the only daughter of the only daughter of her only daughter will arrive in time for Juneteenth, accompanied by your mother and two brothers, and that we accept the kind invitation to stay with her and James."

"We're not staying in a motel?" Steven asked with a groan. "Surely you jest, Mom!"

Mom just laughed, her old self again, and went back to the kitchen. Of course she was serious—we all knew that. But we had forgotten to ask her who, exactly, James was.

TWO

Closed for Vacation

I THOUGHT IT WAS settled. That night I even called Alicia to tell her we were going. But the next day Mom backed off. "I've been thinking about it," she said, "and I don't know if I can handle it. It's been so long!"

"Of course, you can," Dad reassured her. It was Friday night, the last customers had gone, and Steven had already left to pick up his girlfriend, Samantha. "And it will be good for the kids. They really need this."

"Besides," I said, "I already wrote to Mother Rose and told her we're coming."

Mom gaped at me. "Oh, Emmy, you haven't!"

"This afternoon," I said. Actually, I *hadn't*, but I'd practiced writing that letter so many times in my head it *seemed* as though I'd really done it.

"Well, then," Mom sighed. "I guess that does settle it."

I wrote the letter and took it to the post office myself the next day, before she could change her mind again.

CAFÉ AU LAIT WILL BE CLOSED FOR VACATION
JUNE 9 TO JUNE 23
AU REVOIR ET À BIENTÔT!
—*Chef Suzanne*

THE BUS was scheduled to leave Connecticut on Sunday afternoon. We'd arrive in Dillon Tuesday morning, forty-three hours later.

Dad drove us to the bus station after lunch on Sunday. (He'd made my melted cheese sandwich on bread he'd baked.) Besides our suitcases stowed in the luggage compartment, we each had a carry-on bag with games, books, tapes, plus tape players with earphones. Mom brought a stack of professional chef magazines that she never had time to read, a notebook for the cookbook that she never had time to write, and a cooler crammed with food. Steven carried his new tennis racket. It was pouring rain.

"Special surprise for the Only Daughter," Dad said, slipping a package into my yellow bag. "Do not open until you are *west* of the Hudson River but *east* of the Mississippi."

Then he hugged us all. "Remember all the things we've talked about," he said to us kids. "It's going to be a new experience for you down there." He waited outside the bus in the downpour while we climbed aboard and found seats about halfway back. He stuck his wet face up close to my window, making silly faces at us until the driver put the bus in gear and backed out of the bay. Dad waved and called, "*Au revoir, mes enfants!*" and whatever other French he could think of. Dad doesn't actually speak much French, but he likes to pretend he can.

The bus pulled away, and suddenly my stomach felt squishy. This was my first trip to the South and Dad said it was going to be a lot different in Texas; racial attitudes there were not like in Connecticut. I wondered what that meant.

An hour later we changed buses in New York City. Not until we went through the tunnel under the Hudson and were in New Jersey did I feel as though we were actually on our way to Texas. My stomach settled down. Then I opened Dad's package, a bright yellow three-ring binder with "Jubilee Journey" lettered across the front. The binder was fitted with extra pockets and blank sheets, plus a couple of pens and colored pencils. A foldout map traced our route across the country, ending with a small map of Texas. There was a star pasted next to Dillon. In clear plastic sleeves were a copy of the invitation from Mother Rose and some pages that had been copied from books. I began to read.

Waltzing across Texas: Ethnic and Regional Festivals

Juneteenth—the 19th of June—is celebrated in many African American communities throughout Texas to commemorate the end of slavery. Although Abraham Lincoln signed the Emancipation Proclamation on January 1, 1863, freeing the slaves in those territories still in rebellion against the Union, the proclamation had little immediate effect in the vast area controlled by the Confederacy. Word of their new status did not reach slaves in Texas for another two and a half years. It was not until June 19, 1865, that General Gordon Granger landed at Galveston and sent out an official announcement that the slaves had been freed. African Americans throughout Texas observe the anniversary of the date with church services, picnics, speeches, and various forms of entertainment.

So now I understood what Juneteenth was about. I loved that word: *Juneteenth*. I had tried to look it up at the library, but I couldn't find anything. Leave it to Dad to dig up the facts.

Next was a page copied from an old-fashioned-looking book called *Five Decades of Dillon: A Historian Looks at His Home Town.*

Center Park

By the early 1920s Dillon was a bustling market town with an eye on the future. Cities of comparable size across Texas were developing handsome parks for beautification and recreation, and Dillon was not to be left behind. An area near the town square deemed ideal for just such a civic project was occupied at that time by a group of poorly built and somewhat run-down dwellings occupied by Negroes. In the spring of 1921 the visionary city fathers began to acquire property in the area, known locally as Freedomtown, at the same time relocating the Negroes to newer and better homes in the southeast section of Dillon. Such was the dedication and diligence of the mayor and other elected officials as well as voluntary organizations that within a matter of months all the Negroes had been moved and work begun on Center Park, destined to become the jewel of Dillon.

"Bet there's a lot more to this story," Dad had written across the bottom of the page. "Ask Mother Rose."

But Mother Rose was still forty hours away.

THREE

Bus Ride

THE FORTY HOURS crawled by as if they had no place to go.

We hadn't been on the road long when I learned my first important lesson: Avoid the rest room on the bus. Hold on until the rest stops, which aren't a whole lot better.

The second important lesson: Bring your own pillow. There was no way I could get comfortable enough to sleep right.

The third lesson: Bring your own food.

Before noon of the second day—somewhere in Virginia, I think it was, or maybe Tennessee—our supply of fruit and cheese and crackers had almost run out. We all sat grumpily in a dingy plastic booth at a rest stop. A waitress with frizzy bleached hair stared hard at the four of us and then made us wait a long time for our food. Everybody else was served way before we were, and Mom was afraid the bus would leave without us.

"How come she's so slow?" I asked, wondering if this was what Dad meant about things being different in the South.

"Because she's a bad waitress," Mom snapped. I wondered if that was the real reason, but Mom seemed so annoyed I decided not to say anything.

I had ordered a grilled cheese sandwich, remembering the way Dad makes them: layers of real cheese between thick slices of crusty bread, buttered on the outside and fried slowly until the bread is golden brown and the cheese oozes out when I take the first bite. The object the sour-faced waitress finally slapped down in front of me had one thin slice of rubbery orange cheese smushed between two flabby pieces of white bread with burnt edges. It wasn't even warm all the way through.

"Why do you order grilled cheese, Emmy?" Steven asked. "You always complain about it." He was wolfing down a couple of thin, greasy burgers, and he obviously didn't care. Robby, in his usual picky way, had had nothing but Carr's water biscuits and juice since we left home and refused to order anything but milk. Mom sipped lukewarm coffee and poked at the wilted lettuce in a turkey sandwich. "I thought I was hungry," she said. "I guess I'm not."

"I wonder what Daddy's doing," Robby sighed.

"Fixing things," I said.

"Please," Mom said, "don't say that."

We live in an old house—"a fixer-upper," my dad calls it—near the original downtown part of Northdale. Dad has been building a deck on the back of the house for more than two years, and he still hasn't put up the railing or even gotten around to nailing down all the floorboards. In January he began to strip the purple-flowered paper off the walls of my bedroom, but by June only two walls were done. I had already chosen the exact shade of yellow paint I wanted. I was hoping that in addition to working on the café, he'd finish my bedroom as a surprise, but I knew Mom was afraid he'd start something new.

The other passengers were heading back toward the bus, and we paid for our mostly uneaten food and hurried after them. "How much longer?" I asked Steven, who was following our progress across the country on the map in my "Jubilee Journey" notebook.

"Twenty-two hours," Steven said, and I groaned.

West of Knoxville, Tennessee, a girl about my age climbed on the bus with her mother—I figured it was her mom because they both had pointy noses and hair that was limp as string and the color of an old broom. They sat down right behind the driver. There weren't many passengers on this part of the trip, so I had a seat by myself, with Mom and Robby and Steven spread out on their own seats behind me. After a while the girl came down the aisle on her way to the rest room. She glanced at me as she passed, and I guess I should have warned her, but I didn't. On her way back she stopped next to my seat, seemed to hesitate, and then slid onto the seat beside me. "I'm Bonnie," she said.

"My name's Emily Rose." I'd just started using the Rose part since I got the letter from Mother Rose. "The rest room was really gross, huh?"

She shrugged and pulled an electronic game out of her purse and showed me how to play it. We didn't talk much, but time went by faster while Bonnie was there with her game. Robby came up to see what we were doing. "He's my brother," I explained to Bonnie, and she let him have a turn. When he got tired of that, he went back to sit in the seat behind us with Steven, who was listening to a tape and staring out the window. Loud music leaked out around the headphones.

Bonnie watched Robby go. "Your brother sat down with some colored guy," she said.

"He's my brother, too," I said. "They both are."

"Your *brother*?" She actually gasped.

"Yes. And that's my mother over there."

Bonnie looked where I was pointing. Mom's dark head was bent over *Food Arts*. Bonnie's pale blue eyes narrowed. "You're black," she said accusingly. "You didn't say nothing about that. You don't look black. But you don't look white, neither, come to think of it."

"I'm a double," I said.

Bonnie peered at me suspiciously. "Double what?"

That's what Mom and Dad had taught us to say to anybody who gave us a hard time about being biracial—half black, half white. *Just tell them you're not half anything, you're double. Tell them you've got twice as much history, twice as much culture, twice as much of everything that counts. Tell them your family swims in a terrific gene pool. Tell them your family tree produces the sweetest, most delicious fruit.*

But mostly people don't say anything. Sometimes they stare. Or they might act weird or rude, like that waitress, but they don't usually come right out and say anything to my face. Bonnie's attitude kind of shocked me. "My mom's African American, and my dad's French American," I told her. I had begun adding the French American thing about the time Mom started calling herself Chef Suzanne. I thought it sounded romantic. *Emily Rose Chartier, French American African American.*

"My folks don't believe in that kind of mixing," Bonnie said sternly. "It's sinful."

Sinful! I thought. *Where does she get off saying my parents are sinful?* But before I could tell her off, she added in a nicer way, "I wish my hair was like yours," and reached out to touch it.

My hair is light brown and curly and there's a lot of it. But I absolutely can't stand to have anybody near it. And I was steamed. "Don't touch me!" I growled softly.

Bonnie jumped as though a snake had bitten her, her eyes round as bottle caps. At that exact moment Bonnie's mom started down the aisle to see what Bonnie was up to. She looked me over and figured it out fast. "Git on back up here, Bonnie Jean," she squawked. "Don't you be bothering folks."

"I wasn't," Bonnie whined.

"We were playing her game," I said fake sweetly, "and talking."

"See ya," Bonnie said, sliding out of the seat. She followed her mother without looking back.

I turned around to see Steven snickering.

"Rednecks," he said, peeling off his earphones. "Welcome to the real world. The trouble with you, Emmy," Steven added, "is that you've led a sheltered life."

"Mind your own business," I snapped.

I hate it when Steven lectures me, but this time I did think about what he was saying. My dad teaches math and biology in a private school, and part of the deal is that my brothers and I can go to Silver Hill Country Day for reduced tuition. They make a big thing at Silver Hill about "ethnic diversity"—we celebrate Hanukkah and Christmas and Kwanza and Ramadan—so most of the time I didn't feel weird about being a double. Lots of other kids in that school are doubles, too, and my parents belong to an organization of interracial families that arranges all kinds of activities for us. During Black History Month in February, for instance, we were constantly going to things like concerts of African music and exhibits of baskets made by blacks from the Sea Islands.

So far I'd been pretty lucky, although I have had some other Bonnie-type experiences. When I was six or seven, a new family—white—moved in down the block. It was summertime, and I quickly made friends with the little girl, Jennifer, who had a backyard pool where I loved to hang out. Jennifer invited me to her birthday party at a pizza place, and I was thrilled about that. But after Jennifer's mother came around and met my mom, she called and said she was sorry, but she could take only six children in her van, and I couldn't go. I begged Mom to drive me to the pizza place, but Mom said, "No, Jennifer's parents are rude people." Instead she got a sitter for Robby and took me to a movie. That was the end of hanging out at Jennifer's pool and the end of our friendship. Jennifer's family eventually moved away, and I learned to be on guard when I first met people until I was sure they understood.

Steven has warned me over and over that the "sheltered life," as he calls it, will end when I leave Silver Hill after eighth grade next year and start high school at St. Pius. "Enjoy childhood while you can," he's advised me. "In high school you won't fit in with any of them, blacks or whites. You're not black enough for the blacks—*I'm* not even black enough for some of them. Remember when those guys at Northdale High School beat me up because they said I was acting white? And no matter what, you'll never be white enough for the whites. You'll find out, Emmy. It's a different world, even at St. Pius."

I did remember when the black guys beat up Steven and how upset Mom and Dad were. They went to talk to the principal, even though my brother begged them not to. The principal told them it was up to Steven to learn to deal with "racial differences." That's when they decided to send him to Catholic school. I was already worried about how I'd deal with that different world when I got to St. Pius. I'd been hoping it would be easier for a girl, but now I wasn't so sure.

In a little town out in the middle of nowhere Bonnie and her mother got off the bus. It was raining hard. They hurried toward an outdoor phone booth, splashing through puddles. The bus pulled away and left them there, huddled in the phone booth. For a moment I spitefully imagined them trapped inside with the booth filling with water. *Glub glub!*

We changed buses in Memphis and choked down another dismal meal. The waiter was black, and there were no problems aside from the bad food. The new bus rolled through the moonless night. I finally managed to fall asleep, glad we'd be in Dillon in the morning but uneasy about it, too. In some way I couldn't quite figure out, it seemed as though a whole new part of my life was about to begin.

FOUR

Welcome Home

MOTHER ROSE?"

She heard the gentle voice from a great distance. First she thought it was Ned wanting her to wake up and being careful not to startle her. But Ned had been gone to Glory fifteen years now, dead in her arms the night of their golden wedding anniversary. She'd never forget *that* night, no indeed! Then she thought it might be Charley, taken from her by sickness before he reached his eleventh birthday. Or maybe it was her brother Henry on the night the white boys tarred and feathered him: *Rose Lee, help me. . . .* So long ago.

She sighed and lay still.

"Mother Rose, you awake yet?" The voice was less gentle, closer.

Mother Rose opened her eyes. Her cousin's face hovered above her, a dark moon with a silver halo. "James," she said.

"They'll be here soon," he said. "The folks from Connecticut. You said you wanted to meet their bus."

"Uh-*huh*," she grunted. "I'll be ready."

James nodded and went away.

Her joints were so stiff she wondered if they'd bend. Somehow they always did. Mother Rose sat up and reached for her robe, poked her feet around the floor for her scuffs. Her heart fluttered in the frail cage of her chest, and she waited for it to slow and settle to its rhythmic tapping. Then she pushed herself up from the bed and shuffled toward the bathroom.

An hour later she sat in the front seat of James's somber black car, dressed in her navy blue Sunday dress with the white collar, her cotton stockings, which were cooler than the nylon ones, and her black shoes. At one time she would have worn a hat to go out, but no one did now except for church. Too late she realized that her glasses were smudged. "I won't be able to see them right," she complained.

James reached over and unhooked the glasses from her ears, blew on each thick lens, and polished them with the white handkerchief from his breast pocket. Then he set them back on her nose. "Better?"

"Thank you."

They waited. She had taken only a little breakfast: tea with milk, a slice of buttered toast, a small glass of juice to wash down the line of pills. The bus was due at eight-thirty, Susan had written. "I hope I didn't get it wrong," Mother Rose murmured.

"You didn't. I checked."

There were other things to worry about. "Do you think we got enough food? Boys eat so much." She smiled, remembering how much Charley used to eat. Then she remembered back much further, to her brother Henry. *Boy must have a hollow leg,* her father used to say.

"Plenty," James said. "Eggs, bread, a gallon of milk, three chickens for tonight's dinner. And we're not far from a store." He patted her knee with his large hand. A gold ring with a red stone shone on his finger. "Everything's ready, don't you worry. Cot set up in the blue bedroom, extra towels laid out, everything. Look—here comes the bus."

James got out—a big man, shaped like a barrel, but quick moving—and came around to open the door for her. She gave him her hand and stepped out cautiously, feeling for the ground. *Need to see that eye doctor*, she thought. The bus door wheezed open, and a couple of young white fellows leaped down. *The children couldn't be that white, could they? Even if Susan married white?* But the fellows left without even glancing at her and James.

Then she saw the two boys—one light, one dark, so handsome—and knew right away. Her eyes clouded with joyful tears. Next she recognized Susan, their mother, tall and fine looking like her daddy. Was Julian Pratt still alive? She couldn't remember. She had lost track of him after Emily died and he married that stupid woman with all the children and took Susan and Ben up north. *Not a bad man*, she thought. *Handsome, but weak. Emily was always the strong one in that couple.*

Close behind Susan came the girl, Emily Rose. Mother Rose thought she saw in the girl such a strong likeness to her own child, even smiling her own Emily's shy smile, that the old woman's heart swelled painfully and the tears squeezed past her will not to cry.

Emily Rose hesitated for just a moment and then walked straight toward her. Mother Rose opened her arms to embrace them all. "Welcome home, children," she said.

FIVE

Uncle James

SHE'S SO TINY!" Robby whispered to me from the backseat of Uncle James's big black Lincoln. "I didn't expect her to be so little, did you? She's like a doll. Or a bird. And she's so *old*!"

"*Shhhhh*," Mom breathed, leaning back on the plush gray seat with her eyes closed. The last couple of hours on the bus she'd picked off practically all the nail polish she'd spent so much time putting on the morning we left. ("The last time I wore nail polish was when your dad and I got married," she'd confided while we were both doing our toenails.) Then when Mother Rose hugged her, she started crying, and now she had just managed to stop.

I hadn't any idea what Mother Rose would

look like, because Mom didn't have a picture of her. So when I first saw her at the bus station, it was kind of a surprise. She probably didn't weigh even a hundred pounds. Her arms and legs were like bones covered with crinkly brown leather. Her wispy gray hair was pinned back in a bun. Her dark skin was crisscrossed with thousands of tiny lines, like a winter leaf. Thick glasses magnified her eyes and made them sort of scary, but her smile was warm.

Mother Rose sat up front next to Uncle James. I could barely see the top of her head from where I sat between Mom and Steven. Robby perched on a jump seat that folded down from the back of the driver's seat. The air conditioner hummed. Uncle James drove.

"Is this his car?" Robby asked, too loud, and Mom shushed him again and nudged him with her foot.

I was wondering the same thing. "I'm James Prince," the man in the pinstripe suit had said, shaking hands with each of us. He wore glasses, too. "My late mother, Lord rest her soul, was Mother Rose's aunt Susannah. Therefore Mother Rose is my first cousin, and I am your cousin thrice removed. However, you may call me Uncle James."

I didn't understand exactly what "thrice removed" meant, except that he was a relative.

Other than that, we didn't know much about James. He had a luxurious car, and I wondered if their house would be luxurious, too. I studied the back of Uncle James's head. It sat on top of a thick neck that bulged up out of his white shirt collar. His hair covered his head like a woolly gray cap.

Uncle James drove us right through the middle of Dillon—past a pink stone courthouse with turrets on each corner and a statue of a soldier holding a rifle, past stores and office buildings, and under a railroad trestle. Now we were in a neighborhood of small, neat houses. Then we turned into a broad driveway that curved up to a white house with a row of stately columns across the front and black shutters at the windows. The house was surrounded by a velvety green lawn and beds of red and purple flowers edged in white. It *was* a luxurious place!

But then, in the middle of the flowers, I saw a sign with ornate lettering: PRINCE FUNERAL HOME & CHAPEL, INC., and below that in plain letters, JAMES PRINCE, FUNERAL DIRECTOR.

"Mom, look!" I pointed at the sign. We all stared. Mom's mouth opened and closed again, and she patted my arm. Steven barely managed to muffle a laugh.

"We're not staying here, are we?" I whispered. There was no way I was going to sleep in any funeral home. I imagined dead bodies stacked all around, some in coffins, some not. This was too creepy to think about, but I could see by the grin on Steven's face that he was loving it. Robby's eyes were wide, and he'd already opened his mouth when Mom nudged him again.

The car glided to a stop under a canopy at the side entrance, and a thin man in a dusty black suit appeared and opened the doors of the car. "This is my assistant, Mr. Phillips," Uncle James explained. "Todd, these people are Mother Rose's relations from Connecticut." Uncle James had a deep, mellow voice; he pronounced each letter in *Con-nect-i-cut*, including the *c* in the middle. Mr. Phillips smiled and bowed to all of us. His narrow mustache looked as though it had been painted on his lip.

Uncle James took charge of helping Mother Rose out of the front seat, and we all scrambled out of the back. It was still early morning, not even nine o'clock, but it was already steamy hot. Mr. Phillips got our bags out of the trunk and helped Steven carry them inside.

Uncle James held the door open, and we stepped into a cool hallway with wood paneling and green carpet and doors with stained-glass windows. Organ music was playing softly in the background. I grabbed Mom's hand, and Mom squeezed mine tight. I could see she was squeezing Robby's hand, too—not just to reassure us but to warn us: *Don't say anything, keep quiet; we'll talk later—don't say* A *WORD!*

"This is my place of business," Uncle James explained, waving his hand to include the paneling and carpet and stained glass. "Our residence is in the rear."

We followed Uncle James and Mother Rose down the quiet hall. I was craning my neck for a look at any bodies that might be lurking behind the stained-glass doors, half afraid I would actually see one. Then Uncle James unlocked a plain door marked PRIVATE, and we entered an ordinary apartment.

Once he'd shut the door behind us, you would never guess that you were in a funeral home. There was a living room with a sofa and a TV, and beyond it a cheerful kitchen with goose-print curtains and a brass lamp hanging over a big round table.

"Allow me to show you to your rooms upstairs," Uncle James said.

We followed him up the carpeted stairs to the second floor. He pointed out his "personal quarters" at the head of the stairs, and we got a glimpse of more dark wood and green carpet like his "place of business." Down the narrow hall were two more bedrooms, one with a double bed for Mom and me, a tiny room crowded with a single bed and a cot for Steven and Robby, and a bathroom in between. Mr. Phillips hauled our bags up the stairs and disappeared.

"Nothing elaborate," Uncle James said in that mellow voice, "but I trust you will be comfortable."

"But where's Mother Rose's room?" Robby asked.

"Mother Rose has her personal quarters downstairs," Uncle James replied. "It makes it easier for her. Please come down and join us for breakfast when you've had a moment to collect yourselves."

The room where Mom and I were to stay was painted yellow, my favorite color, and there was a pretty flowered bedspread on the old-fashioned bed and some framed pictures of flowers hanging on the walls. I pushed aside the ruffled white curtains and peeked out the window. It overlooked the driveway behind the funeral home and faced a three-car garage. A long black hearse was parked in front of the garage.

Before I could say anything to Mom about the hearse, Robby and Steven rushed in from checking out their room. "Mom!" Robby said excitedly. "Did you see what's out there? Steven says there's a body in it."

"We are not going to discuss it!" Mom snapped, impatiently cutting him off. "There's nothing to be frightened of. James performs a useful service. Just *deal* with it, OK?"

"I wasn't going to say anything bad," Robby protested. "I was just going to say that I think it's neat, staying here. Maybe Uncle James will show me how to stuff a body."

"They don't stuff them," Steven said. "They embalm them. Actually it could be quite interesting. You'd find it interesting, wouldn't you, Emmy?"

"Umhmm." If I was the only one who was scared, I sure wasn't going to let on in front of my brothers.

"We can unpack later," Mom said. "I'm feeling too frazzled to do it now. Let's wash up, and then we'll go downstairs and have breakfast."

While Robby and Steven were in the bathroom, I took another look out the window. Mr. Phillips had taken off his jacket and was getting ready to wash the hearse. I didn't think he'd wash it if there was a body inside. That wouldn't seem right.

Downstairs, Mother Rose was sitting at the table, a newspaper spread out in front of her. Uncle James was reading over her shoulder. "Look at this," he said, and we crowded around them.

TWO BLACK CHURCHES TORCHED IN GREENVILLE, the headline screamed above a color picture of a big fire. "That's only about seventy-five miles from here," Uncle James said. "Last week it was a church up in Oklahoma. Seems the fires are getting closer."

Mother Rose sighed. "Seems like all that old anger and hatred is boiling up again. Reminds me of when I was a girl and our school burned down. All our people were at a meeting with the white folks, finding out again just how much we weren't wanted anywhere in Dillon, and then Professor Prince—he'd be James's daddy some years later—well, he came running in yelling that the school was on fire. We tried, but there was nothing could be done to save it. And we all knew somebody had set that fire. Somebody that hated us enough to destroy what was dear to us. Just like somebody hates those folks over in Greenville."

"Did they catch the people that burned your school?" Robby asked.

"They did not," Mother Rose replied. "But I have faith that the police will be more successful now than they were back then."

Then Uncle James, who had a white apron covering his broad front, rubbed his hands briskly and said, "The reason they didn't catch anyone seventy-five years ago was that they didn't *try*. Now—maybe some breakfast would be a good idea. Bacon and eggs sound good to you folks? Some grits and homemade biscuits?"

"Oh, I haven't had grits in years!" Mom said.

I didn't know what grits were, but I found out when Uncle James served up a bowl of something that looked like Cream of Wheat with a lump of butter melting in the middle. It was delicious. Mom made herself a biscuit-and-bacon sandwich. "This was my favorite breakfast when I was growing up," she said dreamily. "My momma made the best biscuits."

Mother Rose smiled at us and sipped her tea with milk, occasionally breaking off a crumb of biscuit. "Tell me about your trip," she said to Steven. She'd put him on one side, Robby on the other, Mom and me across from her. Uncle James hovered around, drinking coffee from a mug and bringing more food when it looked as though we were running low.

"It was *long*, forty-three hours," Steven said. "And pretty boring."

"It wasn't that bad," my mother protested mildly. "I thought it would be a good way to see the country."

"The food," I said, "was the worst. It was really awful."

"The toilets!" Robby almost shouted. "You can't believe how nasty they were. They *stank*. Pee-yeewwww!"

Mom fixed him with a glare. "Not good table talk, Rob."

Mother Rose only smiled some more. I wondered if those were her real teeth. "And your poppa?" she asked, peering at me through her thick glasses. "Gilbert wasn't able to come with you?"

"He's working," I said. "At the nature center. When I go home I'll be a junior curator. I'm old enough."

Mom told her about the center and about Silver Hill where Dad taught. That led to Café au Lait.

"The restaurant is named for us kids," I explained. "Because we're doubles, both black and white." I wondered if she'd think that was a dumb thing to say.

"And what kind of food do you serve at your café?" Mother Rose wanted to know, skipping past the black-and-white part, and when Mom described some of the specialties, like *coq au vin* and *boeuf bourguignonne*, Mother Rose shook her head. "James, what these children need"—she waved her hand to include Mom as one of the children—"is some of your fried okra and peach cobbler."

"Of course," Uncle James agreed. "And they will be getting plenty of that at the Juneteenth Jubilee."

"I know what Juneteenth is!" I announced. "Dad found out for us. It's the anniversary of the day the slaves in Texas learned they were free at last."

"Good for you!" Mother Rose said. "Black folk have been celebrating Juneteenth for years and years now, except for a while when young people didn't want to be reminded that once upon a time we were slaves. But this year is special, you know—the Diamond Jubilee, to recall the last days of Freedomtown seventy-five years ago. Did your poppa find out about Freedomtown for you, too, Emily Rose?"

I loved the way she said my name, as though each syllable was very precious. "He found out how it ended," I said. "White people took it away from the black people." I felt funny saying "white people" and "black people," as though they were different from me, instead of me being both.

"The ending is the sad part," Mother Rose said. "The beginning and the middle of the Freedomtown story were good." She peered into her empty cup, and right away Uncle James brought the kettle and filled her cup with hot water. Mother Rose carefully dunked her soggy tea bag. Then she reached for a pitcher shaped like a cow and slowly poured milk into the tea. Just as slowly she scooped in a teaspoon of sugar and stirred and stirred. It was almost as if she had forgotten we were there.

"Tea-o-lay," she said with a little smile, "is that what you would call it?" She looked around at us, her eyes shining behind her glasses. "Now," she said, "let me tell you the story of Freedomtown. It's my story, and so in a way it's your story, too."

Mother Rose's bright eyes traveled around the table and settled on me. "In the time before we knew that we would be driven away, our lives uprooted, and our people scattered," she began, "Grandfather Jim Williams spent every spare minute tending his beautiful garden in Freedomtown."

Mother Rose described the Garden of Eden that her grandfather had created around his old home in Freedom. We were caught up in the spell of her story, enchanted by her soft, musical voice.

"I was a girl just about your age, Emily Rose, when I found out that the white people in Dillon wanted that land for a park. I was serving a fancy lunch to some white ladies at Mrs. Eunice Bell's big mansion, and I was having the worst time you can ever imagine, trying to figure out which plates and bowls were supposed to go where. And these ladies, members of the Garden Club, were discussing their plans to move the

Negroes out of Freedomtown. I was setting their soup down right under their noses, but to them I was just a little old colored girl, with no more ears to hear or brains to understand than that clock on the wall yonder!

"When my work was finished, I walked home with Grandfather Jim, and we went straight to my poppa's barbershop and told his customers, all the influential men in our neighborhood, what I'd heard. They asked me a lot of questions, and then they all began to talk and discuss what could be done, how they were going to get together and fight this. Didn't I feel important! Then my momma came to get me, because I had failed to go straight back to the kitchen and was lingering in the barbershop like I wasn't supposed to, and I told her what I'd heard. Momma pulled her apron up over her face and wept in front of all those men, and I felt so bad for her, I started in crying, too. Oh my, that was a sad day."

That story made us all feel bad.

"I don't see," Steven said angrily, "how they could just make all of you move. Wasn't that illegal?"

"White folk made the laws to suit themselves, Steven," Mother Rose said. "Lots of people in Freedom, like my poppa, wanted to circulate a petition against us being moved, but my brother

Henry, who was always stirring up trouble, insisted that it would never work. He said the whites wouldn't pay any attention to a bunch of Negro signatures. He argued for a work stoppage."

"He sounds just great," Steven said. "A real radical."

"That he was," Mother Rose agreed. "Got himself tarred and feathered for that, and he was headed for much worse. You went against the white man in those days, and you might not come out alive. The only way to survive was to give in or get out."

"Tarred and feathered?" Steven asked. "You mean they actually *did* that to your brother?"

"Sure did. Smeared him all over with hot tar and covered him with chicken feathers. I never saw anything so horrible in my life. It took my momma hours to get that mess off of him, and he was burned pretty bad. He was bandaged up for a good long time."

I shuddered, thinking about poor Henry. Mom closed her eyes, and I could see Steven's hands balling into fists.

After these terrible stories, Mother Rose added more milk to her almost empty cup and told us a story that made me feel warm inside. "Do you know, Emily Rose, who you're named for?"

I answered, "For you, and for my grandmother Emily."

"That's right, but only partly so," Mother Rose said. "One day, not long after that Garden Club lunch, I was in Mrs. Bell's garden, helping Grandfather Jim. A white lady came by—I recognized her from the lunch—and asked if she could do a sketch of me and my grandfather. And Lord, I don't to this day know what got into me, but I just burst out, 'I like to draw, too,' and I had the nerve to show my drawings to this white lady artist. Her name was Miss Emily Firth. You know what she said?"

I shook my head, so excited I could hardly talk.

"She said, 'You are very talented, Rose Lee,' and then Miss Emily Firth promised to give me drawing lessons."

I could have listened for hours to stories of Freedomtown, even the awful ones, and we were at the table so long that Uncle James began setting out bread and cold cuts for lunch. After a while Mother Rose said, "There's much more to tell, but we do have plenty of time, and I'm tired now. I think I'll go rest myself for a bit, if you will excuse me." She pushed herself up out of her chair and made her way back to her personal quarters. The door closed quietly. Uncle James disappeared, taking the newspaper with the story of the fires with him. So now there was just the four of us at the table.

"She's like a history book," Steven said. "Mother Rose remembers everything way, way back."

"'Cause she's so *old,*" Robby said.

"You'll be old, too, in another seventy-five years," I told him. "You'll be eighty-five."

And I'll be eighty-eight years old, just one year older than Mother Rose. I tried to imagine myself that old, sitting at a table with my great-grandchildren and telling them stories about what life was like when I was a kid. I'd have to start doing a better job of paying attention, I thought, so I'd remember the important things to tell them, just like Mother Rose was telling us.

Then I looked across the table at Mom. She was crying again! "You know what?" she said shakily, trying to smile. "All I need is a hot bath and a nap, and I'll be a whole new person. You'll see."

But what I was seeing *was* a whole new person, or at least a Susan Pratt Chartier I'd never seen before.

SIX

Exploring

THE IDEA, according to Uncle James, was to wait until early evening, when the worst of the heat would be over, and then to explore the part of Dillon that had once been Freedomtown. The question was what to do with ourselves for the next few hours.

Mom went upstairs to take a long bath and a nap. Mother Rose was probably asleep in her room. Uncle James announced that he had work to do that would keep him occupied until dinnertime. The first thing I thought of was, *What kind of work is he doing?* But naturally I didn't say anything.

And naturally Robby just came right out with whatever was in his mind. "Uncle James, before you go to work," he asked, "would you show us where you stuff the bodies?"

Steven snickered and poked me with his elbow, and Uncle James looked as though he'd just been tossed a basketball that he didn't quite know how to handle. "To begin with," he said, "bodies aren't stuffed. They are embalmed. A surgical procedure is used to inject a special fluid into the veins of the dead body. I can't show you that, but there are some things I can show you young folks, yes, indeed."

I decided that this kind of tour might be pretty interesting, as long as bodies weren't included.

First Uncle James opened a pair of carved wooden doors to a big room with formal-looking chairs and sofas and a couple of tables with brass lamps. Sunlight filtered through the curtains and glowed on the striped wallpaper. Organ music was still playing. It reminded me of Grandma Chartier's living room in Wisconsin.

"This is the slumber room," Uncle James said, "where the deceased lies in repose to give friends and relatives an opportunity to view the body and to express their condolences to the bereaved. Now let me show you our chapel. We're especially proud of it, because I designed it myself for maximum flexibility as well as beauty. We believe that beauty is a great comfort to the bereaved at such a time."

It looked like a church—not St. Brigid's where we go every Sunday, with its crucifix above the altar and beautiful statues of saints and dozens of candles, but plain like First Presbyterian, where my friend Alicia goes.

The phone rang in Uncle James's office across the hall, and he excused himself and hurried to answer it. We waited around, listening to the muffled rumble of Uncle James's deep voice on the other side of the closed door. Then the door opened and Uncle James stepped out, buttoning his jacket. "We've just received a call," he said. "I'll have to get back with you young folks later."

We followed Uncle James outside. The heat hit us like a blast from Mom's professional-size oven. Uncle James walked quickly around to the back of the building, where Mr. Phillips was now polishing the hearse. The long side windows were draped with gray velvet, and a sign in each window spelled out PRINCE FUNERAL HOME & CHAPEL, INC. in silvery letters. Steven walked right up and peered in. Robby and I kept our distance.

"We have a removal at Sunset View," Uncle James told Mr. Phillips. "But first I'd better have a word with Mother Rose," he added, and hurried back inside, leaving us standing there.

"So how're you folks doing?" Mr. Phillips asked us. He was still dressed in his white shirt and black pants with black suspenders, and he was rubbing away at the chrome with a rag that looked as clean and white as his shirt.

"Fine, thank you," I mumbled.

"It's *hot*!" Robby complained, puffing out his cheeks. I thought of the big maple in our backyard, where Dad had helped us build a tree house. It always seemed cooler in the tree house.

Mr. Phillips nodded, carefully folded his polishing cloth. "Some say Texas summers are the worst," he said. "Not as bad here, though, as down around Port Arthur, where my wife's from." He retrieved his black jacket from the front seat of the hearse, pulled a black necktie out of the pocket, and put it on.

In a few minutes Uncle James was back. "We should be gone about an hour," Uncle James informed us. "Think you can entertain yourselves in the meantime?"

We nodded.

"What's a removal?" Robby asked.

Uncle James adjusted the cuffs of his shirt and straightened his tie. "It means we're picking up the remains of an elderly gentleman who passed away this morning," he explained. "I just received the call from the nursing home. Then I must meet with the bereaved to make funeral arrangements."

"Who was it?" Steven asked.

Uncle James looked startled. "Mr. Cornelius Overton," he said. "A prominent businessman in our community. A fine gentleman."

Mr. Phillips had backed a windowless van out of the garage. We watched Uncle James hoist himself into the passenger seat, and the van drove slowly down the driveway.

"Come on, guys," Steven said as soon as the van was out of sight, "let's go back inside. We've got a whole hour. We can check it out ourselves. I'm *dying* to have a look around," he added, grinning.

"Huh-*uh*," I said, ignoring his stupid joke. "Not me." Robby didn't want to, either, until Steven pointed out that if we waited for Uncle James to come back, there would be an actual body on the premises.

Since there was no way I wanted to see that body, I let myself get talked into it. I tiptoed behind Steven with my nerves pulled tight, not even knowing what I was scared of. Steven led the way down the hall from the chapel and opened the next door he came to. I let out a scream. Not a very loud one, but I was just not expecting to see an entire roomful of coffins.

Some of the caskets were wood, and some were metal. The lids stood open so you could see the satin linings and the satin-covered pillows and matching blankets. One corner of the big room was curtained off with a blue drape held up by little gold-and-white angels to display several small white coffins, which I guessed must be for children.

I was looking at those coffins and feeling sad that sometimes even little kids die when I heard an eerie sound, like a moan. I whipped around. For a second I thought my brothers had left me alone in that spooky place, and I was about to freak when I glanced at the biggest, fanciest casket, the one in the center of the room on a kind of platform. There was Steven, *lying in the casket*, his eyes closed and his arms crossed over his chest. "*Oooooooh*," came the moan again, courtesy of Robby, crouched behind the coffin.

"Steven!" I yelped. I was both scared and mad, and I did what I always do when I'm scared and mad—I started to cry. "You are *despicable*!" I wailed. "*Loathsome*," I added.

"OK, OK," Steven said, climbing out. "Only teasing." He plumped up the little pillow and smoothed the blanket. At least he had had the sense to kick off his sneakers before he got in there. "Did you see the price tags on these puppies?" Steven asked as he knelt to tie his laces.

"No, I did not," I said.

"Stiff," he said. "Get it? *Stiff*. It's a pun."

I still didn't get it.

Steven is always exasperated when he has to explain his jokes. "A price that's very high is said to be stiff. Also, *stiff* is another word for a corpse, because dead bodies are stiff. Now do you get it?"

"Yes. But I don't think it's funny."

"The point is," Steven went on, "that it seems to be pretty expensive to die around here. A funeral costs thousands of dollars. I'd rather spend that money while I'm still alive—on a car, for instance. That coffin I was in? It's called the Monarch." He held up both hands, fingers spread. "Ten big ones," he said.

"I just want to get buried under the tree in our backyard," Robby announced. "Where we put Foggy." Foggy was our dog who got hit by a garbage truck a year or so ago. Dad dug a hole, and we wrapped Foggy in an old blanket and had a funeral for him.

Steven was already peering into another room, which turned out to be a storage closet filled with folding chairs. Then he yanked open the next door, fumbled for a light switch—and stopped in his tracks.

"Wow," Steven breathed. "Wait till you guys see *this*!"

Robby and I crowded into the doorway of what looked like an operating room on TV. It had no windows and was dimly lit, but I could make out a big metal table gleaming in the center. Near the table was a glass cabinet with steel instruments. Large hooks and pulleys dangled from the ceiling. A black rubber apron hung near the door. I shuddered.

"I bet this is where they do . . . whatever it is they do to you when you're dead," Robby whispered.

Steven cleared his throat. "The embalming room," he said. He stepped inside the room and walked over to the metal table.

"Steven," I said carefully, "if you have *any* ideas in your head about getting up on that table—"

We all heard the car engine. Then a car door slammed, and we realized that there was something like a garage door in the opposite wall. For a couple of seconds we were practically paralyzed. Then, just as the garage door started to rise, we turned and ran. Steven shut the inside door behind us quickly. We listened behind the door as the van backed up closer. "Good, Todd, hold it right there," Uncle James said. We heard the squeak and thump of wheels in the embalming room and the rattle of chains and a pulley and another thump as though something heavy had landed on the metal table. Something like a dead body.

"That must be Mr. Overton," Steven said.

Whoever it was, that was it for me. I rushed down the hall with my brothers at my heels. We burst through the door marked PRIVATE and hurled ourselves into Uncle James's kitchen, exploding with nervous giggles.

Mother Rose sat at the table, sipping a cup of tea. "Good afternoon," she said, regarding us with a calm smile. "Have you been exploring?"

SEVEN

Grudge

MOM CAME DOWN from her nap dressed in white shorts and a green shirt, and she did look fresh and relaxed. I should mention that my mother is very attractive. She is tall and slender, and even though she's around food all the time, she never seems to gain weight. She had her long, dark hair tied back with a green silk scarf. Her skin is a delicious color, like nutmeg. The first thing you notice about Mom is her smile. She claims she inherited her beautiful white teeth from her father, Grandpa Pratt.

Mother Rose beamed at her. "You look refreshed," she said.

"I do feel better," Mom replied. She sat at the table next to Mother Rose and reached for her knobby hand. "It's so good to be here," she said. "I just wish I'd come sooner. Years ago."

"But you're here now; that's what counts," said Mother Rose.

I plopped down across from Mom. Robby had turned on the TV in the living room, and Steven was moving around restlessly, peering out of the windows, opening and closing the refrigerator.

"Are you hungry?" Mother Rose asked. "James will fix us some dinner as soon as he finishes his work. Cornelius Overton crossed over. He's been failing for some time."

"Uncle James says he was a prominent citizen," Steven said, interrupting his nervous cruise around the kitchen.

"There are those who think so," Mother Rose snapped. We all looked up, surprised at her sharp tone.

"Sounds like you don't quite agree with that," Mom said.

Mother Rose sighed. "It's sinful of me to carry a grudge for so many years," she said. "But it seems that people in this community have short memories. My memory goes back a long way. I recollect when we were told we had to leave Freedomtown; to pacify us, the city offered to hire mules to drag our houses out to a nasty old place called The Flats, right by the city's open cesspool. You'd never know it now, but that's what this part of town was like back then—ugly and smelly! Everybody in Freedom was upset. Lots of black folk started leaving Dillon, thinking it had to be better almost anyplace. My best friends were packing up to get *out* of there.

"Except, I recall clearly, Gus Alexander, who had an important job as foreman at the brickyard. Gus thought he was in good with the mayor, who happened to own the brickyard. Gus was the first man to get his house moved out to The Flats, bad as it was in those days. And then what do you know, he started building a nice brick addition to his house!"

Her hands gripped the edge of the table. Steven had stopped pacing and settled down to listen to Mother Rose's story.

"Then," she continued, "up from Fort Worth comes Mr. Gus Alexander's brother and sister and in-laws and all their children, including a poor foolish girl named Ella who took my job serving at Mrs. Bell's. Not that she wasn't welcome to the privilege, far as I was concerned."

Robby, who had gotten bored watching TV and now sat listening to Mother Rose, asked suddenly, "But who's the guy in there?" He jerked his head in the direction of the room where I imagined Mr. Cornelius Overton lying on the cold metal table.

"I'm getting to him. That's Ella's first cousin, Cornelius. Corny, we called him. Corny is the last one of that generation. See, it was Ella who told on Catherine Jane and me. Catherine Jane is Mrs. Eunice Bell's daughter. Even though she was white and a few years older and I worked for her mother, we were friends. Catherine Jane was the only good person in her family, in my opinion. I've always believed her brother, Edward, was part of the bunch that tarred and feathered Henry. Maybe she knew about it, but there was nothing she could do. Later then, when Henry sassed Edward and refused to wash his car, my poppa was afraid Edward and his friends would whip Henry or even hang him—that sometimes happened, too! So I asked Catherine Jane for help, and she was willing. She borrowed her poppa's car—without permission, it goes without saying—and she and Aunt Susannah hid Henry in the backseat and drove him to safety."

"So he got away," Steven said.

"Yes, but there was a price," Mother Rose went on. "Catherine Jane refused to tell her momma and poppa where she'd gone in their car, or why. But Corny's meddlesome cousin Ella couldn't wait to tell them Catherine Jane had gone off with me, and I imagine they put two and two together. Ella didn't have to do that, but she did. Catherine Jane was forbidden to speak to me. For a while we wrote each other letters, and my aunt Tillie carried them back and forth for us. But we got tired of that. Then years later, after Catherine Jane married, she hired me to come to work for her. I went, because I felt I owed Henry's life to her. In a way, that had bound us forever. Her parents, Mr. Tom and Mrs. Eunice Bell, didn't have *that* to say about it then," she said, and snapped her fingers so loudly it sounded like bone breaking.

"What I don't understand," Mom said gently, "is why you hold it against Cornelius because his cousin Ella tattled on you."

"Well, because Corny was the very same kind of person!" Mother Rose exclaimed, slapping the table. "He'd make up to white folk at the expense of black folk every time, just to put himself forward. The sad thing is, he played Uncle Tom and he got away with it. It runs in the family—his grandson Marcus is on the city council and he's just like his grandfather. You wait and see, Marcus will be at the funeral shedding crocodile tears. I don't trust a one of them. Except now with Corny gone there's one less, no great loss to the world." She patted her mouth, hushing herself. "But I mustn't speak ill of the dead."

Mom got a pitcher of iced tea from the refrigerator and poured us each a glass. "Tell us about Cornelius," she coaxed.

Mother Rose stared into her iced tea, as though she was peering into the past. "Well, when Corny first came to town his momma, Lucille Overton—that would be Gus Alexander's sister—had a business making cosmetics that she cooked up in her kitchen. Skin lighteners, hair straighteners, things of that nature. Oh, how we all did try to look white in those days! Corny would travel all over north Texas, sometimes even up into Oklahoma, peddling Madam Lucille's Amazing Beauty Products. He got so successful that he opened a shop selling all kinds of things besides the beauty products, almost like a little drug store with home remedies and the like. Next, he added a room for groceries. Then, in a year or two, he built a moving picture house for colored folk, since we weren't allowed to go to the ones in Dillon, or if we did it was to sit upstairs in the rickety old balcony."

"Sounds like a shrewd businessman," Mom murmured.

"Oh, shrewd, yes, indeed!" Mother Rose agreed. "But the truth of the matter is, Cornelius

Overton wouldn't have gotten much of anywhere if his uncle Gus Alexander hadn't been cozy with the mayor, who aside from owning the brickyard also owned the bank and decided who got loans and who didn't. You see what I'm saying? The mayor knew he could count on Corny's help if anything came up with the old Freedomtown folks out there in The Flats, with its open cesspool and flies and mosquitoes the size of bats and not a tree in the place big enough to shade a kitten. So Cornelius Overton opens up the Palace Theatre. It wasn't any palace, you can take my word on that, still it was a place us black folk could go, maybe riding in one of the Overton Taxicab Company's taxis, owned by you-know-who, and afterwards if you had the money, to the Stardust Diner for an ice-cream soda, owned by you-guessed-it."

"So why'd you go there, Mother Rose?" Robby asked. "Why didn't you just go someplace else?"

"Because, child, it was the only place in Dillon that would serve Negroes, so we had no choice but to go there. And Corny turned it to his advantage. It wasn't cheap, no sir! Ned took me there on our first real date, I guess you'd call it."

Mother Rose seemed to drift away from us. I

could feel Robby cranking up to ask another one of his direct questions; his body would tense up, and then out would pop whatever came into his curious mind. Mom could sense it, too; she looked hard at Robby and shook her head—*No, Robby, that's enough.*

I myself was wondering about Ned, who I guessed had been Mother Rose's husband, but I kept still. I imagined she was thinking about him and maybe forgetting to be so mad at old Cornelius Overton, because she was smiling a little.

We were all sitting quiet as can be, waiting to see if there was going to be more to the story, when the connecting door from the funeral home opened and Uncle James stepped in, adjusting his gold cuff links. He glanced around the table at the five of us, four spellbound Chartiers and Mother Rose in her dream.

"Well, well, well," he said in his booming voice, "must be about time to get some dinner on the stove. How would y'all feel about some good old-fashioned southern fried chicken?"

That woke us from the spell. "Sounds great," Steven said. Uncle James tied on his spotless white apron.

"Marcus Overton been around?" Mother Rose asked peevishly above the rattle of pans.

"He has, indeed, Mother Rose," Uncle James

said. "He and his sister, Pauline Woodrow. To make a selection and arrange the details."

"Which one did they pick?"

"The Monarch," Uncle James said.

Ten big ones, I thought.

EIGHT

Freedomtown

GOOD CHILDREN, thought Mother Rose, as James's car rolled down the driveway onto Morgan Street after the dinner dishes had been cleared away. *The girl, Emily Rose, seems bright. She'll carry the story. I feared it would be lost, but now I don't think so. Our story will be safe with her.*

The car moved quietly through their neighborhood, the area that used to be called The Flats but was now called Southeast. *That shyster Corny Overton came up with the name*, Mother Rose thought. *Just like him to do that—try to erase the past.*

At least Corny hadn't taken it into his head to rename the streets. They were all there, reminding her of the families who had left:

Ragsdale Avenue, Morgan Street, Webster, Hembry—proud names every one. Williams Street, now sadly run-down, a blight on a nice neighborhood, had been named to honor her own grandfather, because he had been one of the oldest residents of Freedom. There was no Mobley Street, though, no Jefferson Street. The Mobleys and the Jeffersons had stayed in Dillon, and by the time they were going on to Glory, there were no streets left in The Flats that needed names.

"We'll take a little tour of the town first, eh, Mother Rose?" James asked. "To orient our visitors." They passed under the railroad trestle and away from Southeast.

"Fine." It didn't make a bit of difference to her. She had no pressing engagements awaiting her at home—just the infuriating presence of the late Cornelius Overton. She loved the purr of the big car's engine, the comfort of the padded seat, the gentle coolness of the air conditioner as long as it wasn't turned up too high. It sparked a remembrance of her childhood trips around Dillon in Grandfather Jim's wagon, drawn by his old mule, Jojo.

She recalled her journey with her grandfather out to the fairgrounds one Fourth of July, with Aunt Tillie's sponge cakes next to her on the wagon seat. First it was Mr. Bell's Packard that passed them, Catherine Jane waving out the window, and a little later Catherine Jane's brother, Edward, sped by driving his Model T Ford much too fast, stirring up a cloud of choking dust.

That was the day Miss Emily Firth had marched across the speakers' platform and announced boldly through the megaphone: "*I want to talk to you this afternoon about the rights of the Negroes in this community who have served you so faithfully and so well for so many years.*"

That gallant speech cost Miss Emily her position as art teacher at the Dillon Academy for Young Ladies—young *white* ladies, that meant. The school wasn't called that anymore; Mother Rose searched for the new name. *Yes—Dillon Community College.* Just now James was winding slowly through the campus, past handsome brick buildings circled with big old trees and green lawns. Mother Rose understood that many of the students at the school now were black. That made her smile. Dr. Wesley Thompson must be turning in his grave.

She remembered the night she'd had to serve a fancy dinner at Mrs. Bell's—skittery as a water drop on a hot griddle, she was—to this Mr. Big Somebody from the college. As she and her aunt Tillie, the Bells' cook, had huddled at the kitchen door eavesdropping, they heard

Dr. Wesley Thompson say, "The people of Dillon are prepared to rid our city of the blight, to eradicate the squalor, of that area known familiarly as Freedomtown."

Now Mother Rose chuckled softly to herself. The tricks of memory! At this moment she could recall that scene, the exact words he had used (*blight, squalor*), the haughty tone of voice, even what she had served for dinner that night (*fruit cup, roast beef*) seventy-five years ago, but she could not for the life of her think of the names of Susan's two boys, who were at this very minute teasing each other in the backseat. Ned, was that the older one? No, she thought not. The boy did resemble her Ned, in a way. Fine looking. But his name stayed somewhere just out of reach. Emily Rose—now that name she would not forget. Ah, Steven, that was it! And the little one was Robby.

Mother Rose gazed out of the window. Long-legged black girls in shorts strolled the campus, fearless, confident, their hair done up in amazing styles, braids, twisted curls. Not many of the young girls seemed to straighten their hair anymore. *Just as well*, she thought, reaching up to touch her own hair, no longer so thick as it had been when she was young. Ned used to laugh at how she strove to tame her stubborn bush of wiry hair to a sleek, sophisticated marcel wave.

"Yonder is the Bell Library," James was telling his passengers. "Next to it, the yellow brick building with the columns is the oldest building on campus, where the school held its first classes. On the other side of the street is the new Earth Sciences Center."

Now how does he know that? Mother Rose wondered. James surprised her at times with all that he knew, although they had always recognized that he was bright. When he was born Rose Lee had already gone to work as nursemaid to Catherine Jane's girl, Phoebe. Soon there was her baby brother, Tommy, to care for as well. Tommy was a rather sullen child, and it was plain as day that he was not near as smart as Aunt Susannah's boy, James, born within a few weeks of Tommy. Still, years later Tommy Plunkett enrolled at the University of Texas in Austin—no Negroes admitted—while James Prince, who had taught himself to read by the time he was four and could do long division in his head by the age of eight and conjugate Latin verbs before he entered high school, spent a year at mortuary school.

Mother Rose sighed.

The car had arrived at the courthouse square. As James circled it slowly, Mother Rose remembered that Juneteenth celebration in 1921 when she and her kinfolk and friends had marched around Freedom as they always did. Then, without a word or a signal, they left their picnic baskets in the church grove and kept right on marching, out of black Freedomtown and into white Dillon, to this same courthouse square.

Ignoring the white men on horseback who appeared at each corner of the square and stared at them with stone-hard faces, they had marched and sung. Around the courthouse they marched, Aunt Susannah in her flame red dress, red parasol bobbing, Rose Lee clutching her hand, heads held high. *Lift every voice and sing. . . .*

Now. Now they would go to the park. Mother Rose pulled out her embroidered handkerchief and readied herself. She hadn't been here in years, even though they said the Senior Citizens Center had some good programs.

James parked in the lot between the library and the tennis court. On the north side where the old Forgiveness Baptist Church used to stand, little children clambered over red, blue, and yellow playground equipment. Young white boys were tossing one of those plastic disks to a spotted dog. Straight ahead was Hickory Creek, crossed by a stonework bridge with a brass plaque marking the site of what used to be Freedomtown, provided by the historical society for those who didn't remember.

But Mother Rose remembered. She recalled another time in the church grove: "*Remember this, niggers!*" *a hooded man had shouted. And then they all began to yell. Young Rose Lee had put her hands over her ears to shut it out. While the flames swallowed up the wooden cross, the men moved away, melting into the darkness, leaving the cross to burn. . . .*

Mother Rose took a slow breath. "This park," she began, and then faltered, tears stinging her eyes after all these years. She cleared her throat and began again. "All this," she told her great-grandchildren, "was Freedomtown."

NINE

Memory

I DON'T UNDERSTAND what happens to memory when people get old.

Mother Rose sometimes could not seem to remember Steven's name, or Robby's. But then she remembered every detail as she led us on a tour of what used to be Freedomtown and is now Center Park.

Mother Rose walked a bit unsteadily, but she refused to take Uncle James's arm. She stopped in the middle of a ball field, near second base. "This was our house," she said. "Right on this spot where I'm standing. Just a plain little old wooden house needing a coat of paint. And over there, on the other side of the creek where the tennis courts are now, was Grandfather Jim's Garden of Eden. Now if that wasn't the most beautiful garden I have ever seen in my eighty-seven years of life on this earth!" She shook her head and walked on, with all of us trailing behind her. "Never will I forget those houses being moved out of Freedom, pulled by mules and rolled on logs all through the night, all the way out to The Flats."

Next she showed us where the school had been—"Booker T," she called it, for Booker T. Washington—before it was burned down, and then the exact location of the houses belonging to Aunt Tillie and Cousin Cora and her childhood friends who had moved away, Lou Ann Hembry and Bessie Morgan. And where the two churches had stood, and Mr. Taylor's tailor shop and Tolivar's grocery store and the Sun-Up Café—I mean, Mother Rose remembered *everything*.

"I made drawings of all of them," she told us. "Every single one, before they got moved away or torn down. I spent the summer making a whole sketchbook of them."

"Do you still have the book, Mother Rose?" Mom asked.

"No, I do not," Mother Rose said. "I gave it to my brother Henry as a keepsake when he left many years ago. I like to think that Henry treasured that sketchbook. But after he was killed in a mining accident up in Colorado, the book disappeared. Poppa fetched Henry's body back here to bury, but he didn't find the book or didn't think to look for it. The Good Lord knows what ever became of those drawings. Wish I still had them, to tell the truth. But"—she tapped her forehead and smiled—"most of it is still up here."

We detoured around the Senior Citizens Center and headed back to the car, pausing at the spot where Dr. Ragsdale's house used to stand. "The house where I was born," Uncle James said.

"But you weren't born in Freedomtown, were you?" Mom asked. "Hadn't it ceased to exist by then?"

"That is correct. After my mother decided to make her home in Dillon and teach school, she purchased the house the Ragsdales left behind when they went north, and Mother Rose's poppa got that house hauled out to The Flats for her."

"Susannah Jones sold the most beautiful ring to buy it!" Mother Rose said. "And she had the house set down right across the street from ours over on Williams Street. It remains there to this day."

"The only house from Freedom that has survived," Uncle James explained.

"It was the finest house in Freedom," Mother Rose added. "The doctor could afford to build it well. And it was the finest house in The Flats, too. All the others got torn down, one by one, people putting up new things all around it, cheaper things that didn't amount to much. Then I don't know what happened—six or seven blocks of that one street started going downhill, nobody took care and some bad elements started moving in. And still there's that pretty little house stuck right in the middle of all that trash."

"Can we go see it?" Robby asked.

"If you're tired we can save that for another time, Mother Rose," Mom suggested.

"Who says I'm tired?" Mother Rose demanded.

On the way to the old house, Uncle James pointed out a building in a small shopping center, Star Laundry and Dry Cleaning. "My other business," he explained. "I opened it in the early sixties with three secondhand washing machines when the only Laundromat in Dillon had a whites only sign on it." Steven and I looked at each other; we'd read about segregation and Jim Crow laws in the South that kept black people out of restaurants and movie theaters—but Laundromats? The law seemed so stupid. "Now we've got fifty machines and a snack bar and a children's playroom," Uncle James added proudly.

Williams Street, a few blocks farther on, turned out to be about as ugly as Mother Rose said. In the middle of the ugliness was this little old house with the windows boarded up and a sheet of plywood nailed over the front door and graffiti sprayed on the walls. The porch railing was broken, and there were bald patches where the faded white paint had peeled off. It was hard to imagine that this used to be the best house in Freedom.

"I was born in the bedroom in the back," Uncle James said, "and I lived in that house until I left for the service. Momma stayed there until she died, and then I sold it. Now I wish I hadn't." He shook his head. "It's sad, what's become of it."

"Dad would be able to fix that place up really nice," I said. I had a sudden yearning to call him up just to hear his voice and tell him I was fine, we were all fine, but he was right—everything was so *different* here.

My mother laughed. "Well, he'd certainly have some good ideas, that's true."

"Why don't you move it?" Steven asked. I could tell he wanted to get out and inspect the house up close, but Uncle James had taken the precaution of locking the car doors. "I bet it could be a nice place again if you got it away from here. There must be a little piece of ground where you could put it."

"Steven," Mother Rose said, turning to peer at him. She even remembered his name this time. "That's a mighty fine idea. And I'll tell you exactly where that sweet old house needs to go. It needs to go back to where it came from. Back to the park, where Freedomtown used to be. Not exactly the same spot, because the old folks' place is there, and I'm sure they wouldn't like it one bit if we tried to tear their place down like they did to us. But somewhere in that same neighborhood. Wouldn't that be something!" she said, and she clapped her hands.

"Wouldn't that be like stirring up a mess of trouble!" Uncle James muttered, letting the car coast down the street.

"Maybe it's *time* to stir up some trouble, James," Mother Rose said, staring straight ahead as we left the desolate neighborhood and drove to our next stop, the cemetery.

Cemeteries always give me a creepy feeling, but then I had never really *visited* one before. It was even creepier when we drove past a freshly dug grave with a pile of dirt next to it. "Corny's new home," Steven whispered, and Mom frowned at him. Uncle James parked, and

Mother Rose was out of the car before he could get around to open the door for her.

WILLIAMS was carved in big letters on the first gravestone she led us to. Underneath that in smaller letters were JAMES and LILA with the dates they were born and the dates they died. "My grandparents," Mother Rose said. Close by was a stone for JEFFERSON, which included CHARLES and ELVIRA, Mother Rose's father and mother. She wandered on, pointing out others in the family: her aunt Tillie and Theo and Walter, her mother's brothers. The dates under the names were long, long ago, and the letters looked weather-beaten and worn.

"I come here every week or two," Mother Rose said, "to make sure everything's all right, grass is mowed, bushes trimmed. Once I tried to plant a lilac bush, but somehow I never could keep it going, and I don't know why. Never happened to me before."

Uncle James pointed out the Prince family tombstone. Above the name were the words REQUIESCAT IN PACE. "It's Latin for 'May he rest in peace,' " Uncle James explained. "My father loved Latin." Next to his mother, Susannah Jones Prince, and his father, Professor Horace Prince, was the grave of his brother, Reuben. "My brother was killed in the Second World War. I hated it when Reuben left and I couldn't go, too. I was too young to serve. I had to wait my turn for the next war, in Korea."

"Sure made your momma mighty glad, though," Mother Rose said, "that she still had one of her boys safe at home back then. Now here"—she pointed to a low gray tombstone—"these are my sisters, Nancy Lee and Lora Lee. They married brothers, farmed together, brought up thirteen children in the same house. They died within eighteen months of each other. Now the four of them are buried here together. How I still do miss those girls!"

Then we gathered in front of a pink granite stone with a big tree spreading its branches above it. A pair of carved angels faced each other from opposite corners. I read the names:

EDMUND MOBLEY
BORN 1903
LOVED BY ALL, GONE TO GLORY 1981

JOHN HENRY MOBLEY
BORN 1934
RETURNED TO THE ANGELS 1934

CHARLES MOBLEY
BORN 1936
CALLED HOME TO JESUS 1946

I wasn't sure who all those people were, but when I came to the next one, I knew. I went up and traced my fingers over the letters:

EMILY MOBLEY PRATT
BORN 1932
TAKEN TO THE BOSOM OF THE LAMB 1966

Mother Rose had taken out her handkerchief and was dabbing at her eyes. But standing in front of her mother's grave, Mom broke down completely, sobbing out loud. Tears running down my face, I moved closer and put my arm around her waist.

Then I noticed that there was one more name:

ROSE LEE JEFFERSON MOBLEY
BORN 1909

The rest of it was blank. It was shocking to me to see it there, ready, waiting for her.

Mother Rose pointed out a few other graves and then we walked solemnly back to the car and sat quietly for a minute or two, collecting our thoughts. Mine kept going back to Emily Mobley Pratt, my grandmother, and all the questions about her that Mom still hadn't answered.

"Is there anywhere else you'd like to go,

Mother Rose?" Uncle James asked, starting the engine.

"I don't think so, thank you," Mother Rose said. "Anyway, we better be getting on home. The sun will be going down soon, and I don't like the idea of Cornelius being there all by his lonesome. No telling what that old scoundrel might be up to."

Steven and I glanced at each other and then looked away fast, choking back a laugh.

"But Mother Rose," Robby said, "Cornelius is *dead*!"

"Well, of course he's dead!" Mother Rose shot back. "And about time, too."

TEN

Family History

WHEN WE GOT BACK to the funeral home, Mother Rose suddenly seemed very tired and went straight to her room, murmuring, "Good night, sleep well." It was still dusk—not even dark yet.

Uncle James yawned and rubbed his eyes. He told us we were welcome to watch TV in the living room if we wanted to and to help ourselves from the kitchen if we were hungry, and he asked if there was anything else he could do for us before he retired to his quarters. "Busy day tomorrow," he said. "I hope you'll forgive me if I don't spend much time with you tonight."

It was hard to believe we'd just arrived that morning. All of us were exhausted after the long bus trip. Robby could hardly hold his eyes open, and even Steven admitted to being sleepy. "It's only nine o'clock here, but it's eleven in Connecticut," he explained, just in case I was about to tease him about going to bed so early. I wasn't. I was tired, too.

Mom and I put on our pajamas and lay down in the old-fashioned bed. I thought I'd fall asleep right away, but we kept thinking of things to say to each other.

"Do you remember Mother Rose from when you were a little girl?" I asked into the darkness.

"I do remember some things about her. I was seven when Momma died and Daddy took off for Chicago and left Benjie and me with Mother Rose. For about a year she was the one safe thing in my life, the life preserver I clung to. Because first I'd lost my momma, and then I'd lost my daddy. Mother Rose took good care of us, and she told us stories about our momma, how smart she was, the kinds of things she did. I was eight when Daddy married Delilah Watson and came back and got us, and we went to live with him and his new family in Chicago. I cried my eyes out when we left, hanging on to Mother Rose and screaming that I didn't want to go. Daddy promised we'd come back to visit, but I didn't believe him. It seemed like I was losing Mother Rose, too, and I must have sensed that I wasn't really getting my daddy back. I was right about that! Delilah was a jealous woman, and I reminded her of my real mother and she hated that."

"Didn't you come back to visit?" I asked. I pictured a little girl clinging to her grandmother, fighting not to be taken away, and it broke my heart.

"No," Mom said, and it came out like a groan. "When I was growing up there were a lot of kids and never enough money. I promised myself that when I was old enough and out on my own, I'd come back. But then—well, then other things happened, and I didn't." She hesitated, and I wanted to ask, *What other things?* but I made myself keep quiet. This was a lot more than Mom had ever told me about her life. I wanted her to keep on talking, because it seemed to me that the more I knew about my mother, the more I'd know about myself. Suddenly I was afraid. If part of her was lost, then that part of me was lost, too.

Mom's thoughts seemed to move off in another direction. "You know," she said slowly, "sad as I was to lose my momma—and I loved her dearly—when I think back on it now, I wonder how Mother Rose *stood* it. She lost all three of her children, one by one."

I thought of the names on the gravestone: John Henry, Charles, Emily. "What happened to them?" I asked.

"Well, my momma was her firstborn. She arrived a year after Mother Rose married Ned Mobley. Then two years later a boy was born, named John for a brother who had died a long time ago, and Henry for her other brother, the one she's been telling us about. But John Henry died before he was a year old. Next came Charley, and he got infantile paralysis—that's what they used to call polio. Before the vaccine was developed it was a serious epidemic, and lots of kids got it and ended up in an iron lung or crippled or worse. Charley died when he was ten or eleven. So that left Emily."

Mom was quiet for a minute. I held my breath, afraid to move, willing her to go on. Slowly she began telling me about Emily, her mother. "She was a teacher, you know. She taught at the same school where Aunt Susannah—that would be Uncle James's mother—and Professor Prince taught."

"I bet she was a good teacher," I said. Mom often told me how much she admired her mother.

"I bet you're right. Today your grandmother might have become a lawyer, a doctor, or anything she wanted to be. But not in those days—her choices were to teach in a black school or to be somebody's maid or laundress and that was *it*."

"But what about my grandfather?" I asked. I don't remember Grandpa Pratt. He died when I was just a baby and in the hospital getting a valve mended in my heart, and Mom flew out to Chicago to the funeral and back the same day while Dad stayed at the hospital with me. She doesn't talk much about her father, either.

"My father, Julian Pratt, was a very talented man. He was a musician, playing at jazz clubs in Dallas. I don't think Mother Rose quite approved of the match, but Momma married him anyway. Then I came along and next came Benjie. Daddy started driving cabs for Mr. Overton and doing whatever other work he could get. I didn't realize until today how much Mother Rose must have hated it that Daddy worked for Cornelius! But a job was a job. Momma went back to teaching. Then there was the accident, and that ended everything."

"Tell me about the accident," I whispered. I had never heard the whole story.

Mom turned onto her side and reached for my hand. "Nobody ever told me exactly what happened, except that Daddy was probably going too fast and skidded off the road and the car flipped over. They were both thrown out. Benjie and I weren't along—I think we were at Mother Rose's that night. My dad wasn't hurt. He walked miles for help, but by the time the ambulance got her to a hospital, Momma was dead. They said the first hospital turned her away, because she was black, you see."

"They wouldn't let her in the hospital just because she was black? But how could white people be so mean?" Thinking about it made me so angry that I sat straight up in bed.

Mom stroked my back through my pajamas. "That's how it was in the South back then. The races were kept separate—not just movies and restaurants but schools and hospitals, too. From the time you were born until you died, if you were black you just didn't go where white people said you couldn't. Did you notice the cemetery this afternoon? No white people are buried there, and the white cemetery probably doesn't have many blacks. That used to be the law, but now it's just custom. People want to be buried where their families are buried."

Then a thought hit me: *If I die right now, where would I be buried? With the white folk or the black?* But I didn't want to think about that, not right then. I wanted to hear more about my grandmother. I lay back down and snuggled up to Mom. "I bet Grandpa Pratt was awful upset about being turned away from the hospital."

"I'm sure he was. But there was more to it that made it even worse for Daddy. A lot of people said the accident was his fault, that he'd been drinking. I remember him coming home really drunk sometimes, but after the accident he quit completely."

"Do you think it was his fault?" I asked. I understood now why Mom never wanted to talk about any of this. It must have been really hard for her to remember, let alone talk about. Suddenly I worried I shouldn't have even asked her the question.

But she answered immediately. "Do I think it was my daddy's fault that my momma died? Yes, I do. But I forgave him a long time ago. He needed to be forgiven. He always felt so guilty. Maybe marrying Delilah was his punishment."

I knew that Mom never got along very well with her stepmother. "She had the brains of an oyster," Mom said once. "She called me Sugar and I always knew she meant anything but."

Mom continued her story, telling me about her father's funeral, how all five of her stepbrothers and stepsisters and her two half-sisters were there, and how they made Mom feel as though she wasn't a good daughter because she came and left so fast. But Uncle Benjie wasn't there at all because he lives in Germany.

Mom has only one picture of her father, a color snapshot taken of them when she was about five years old. Dad had the picture enlarged and framed for her as a present. In the picture she's hanging over her father's shoulder, her face close to his, and they've both got these huge smiles. He was very handsome, even in that old snapshot. Her little brother, Benjie, stands beside them, not smiling but hanging on tight to his daddy's hand. Mom told us that when her dad got remarried, Delilah made him get rid of all his old pictures of Mom's real mother.

"How come he married Delilah?" I asked my mother. It seemed strange that after Grandpa Pratt had been married to Emily, who was so smart and everything, he had turned around and married a person with the brains of an oyster who sounded like a mean and selfish witch.

"Who knows?" Mom said. "I imagine he thought he loved her. And she wanted a daddy for those five kids of hers as much as he wanted a mother for his two."

We were quiet then, even though there was a lot more I wanted to ask. I couldn't make up my mind whether to try to learn some more or to let it go for now.

In seventh grade I had an assignment to write a biography of "somebody important." I picked my mother as my subject. Here's what I remember of what I wrote, based on what she'd told me:

My mother, Susan Pratt Chartier, was born May 26, 1959, in Dillon, Texas. Her mother died in

1966, and her father married someone else. They lived in Chicago where Susan graduated from high school. She started college as a political science major and held two part-time jobs. She dreamed of being a civil rights lawyer. But when she was working on a voter registration campaign she met another student, Gilbert Chartier, dropped out during her junior year, got married, and had three children. Susan Pratt Chartier owns a restaurant and works long hours but finds time to enjoy swimming, ice skating, reading mysteries, listening to certain kinds of jazz, and watching old movies. She always takes time to listen to us.

What I didn't write was, "She hardly ever talks about herself." I decided to try to learn some more.

"Mom?" I asked. "Are you still awake?"

"Umhmm."

"How come—," I began, and then I started over. "I still don't quite understand why you never came back here to see Mother Rose. After you were grown-up and all."

There was a long silence. I waited. Maybe this was dangerous territory. "Oh, Emmy, life gets so complicated sometimes," she said at last. "I was always putting it off until I'd have enough money—that was a big factor. Then I met your dad. And we got married."

"So why didn't you and Dad come here?" I wondered if maybe it was because Dad was white.

"Well, this was something I was going to tell you later, when you're older, but since you asked, maybe this is the right time." She took a deep breath. "The thing is, I was pregnant when I married your dad. We loved each other very much, but we didn't plan to get married until after we both finished school. And then, well, it happened, that's all. And it was a very, very hard time for us, because when your dad's parents found out about me, that I was black and that I was pregnant, they went bananas. They refused to help your dad anymore with his education, or with anything else. So we were on our own. We both dropped out, and your dad worked in a warehouse and finished college at night after Steven was born."

So that explained it. Poor Mom! I bet Mother Rose would have loved her just as much. I wondered if Steven knew this story. "But what about Grandma and Grandpa Chartier?" I asked fearfully, thinking of the sweet white-haired people who came to visit every other Christmas. "I thought they loved us."

"Oh, they do, honey, they do! But it didn't happen right away. Sometimes it takes people a while to accept changes—changes in what they expect for their kids. But once they got one look at their first grandson, well, it's been fine ever since. They opened their hearts to all of us. There are pictures of you kids all over their house, remember?"

I did, and that made me feel a little better. But I was sure getting a lot to think about. "Then what happened?" I asked.

"Well, your dad finished up his degree when I was expecting you, and he got a teaching job. We didn't have much money, but we managed. Not enough, though, to finance a trip to Texas. And after all those years I guess I just didn't have the courage to go back and open those old wounds—losing Momma; losing Daddy, too, in a way; losing Mother Rose and all the rest of the family that I'd had to leave behind.

"And there was something else: I was embarrassed. I didn't want Mother Rose to know that I'd messed up, getting pregnant, because I knew how much she was counting on me to be like my mother. Get an education. Be somebody. I felt ashamed, like I'd let her down. So I kind of let our relationship slip away. Now, coming here after all these years, I see what a mistake that was. A much bigger one than I'd already made."

"Oh, Mom!" I said, and I reached over and hugged her. We lay there in silence for a long time. I don't know which of us fell asleep first.

ELEVEN

Cornelius

ROBBY AND I were the first ones up Wednesday morning. We found the table set with four places, a pot of coffee in the machine, a pitcher of pancake batter by the stove, syrup and butter on the table, but no sign of Uncle James or Mother Rose. Robby and I are like Dad, who is always up before sunrise, but it's hard to get Mom and Steven moving in the morning.

Mom came down a little later. She smiled and kissed my forehead, but before I could say anything, down came Steven. We were all making pancakes in weird shapes when the door from the funeral home opened and Mother Rose stepped in. She looked around at us, bright-eyed and smiling. "Everybody got a good rest last night?"

"Yes, ma'am," we said.

"There's plenty of coffee, Mother Rose," Mom said. "Would you like a cup?"

"Some tea would be nice," she said, settling in her place at the table. "There's probably still some juice in the tea bag I used earlier. My cup is in the sink."

Mom brought her the cup filled with hot water and the old tea bag. Mother Rose swished the tea bag around. "Been in there taking a look at Cornelius," she said. "Looks better than he ever did when he was alive. Marcus is in there now. I can't bear the sight of that man. Or his rotten-spoiled wife, Aurelia. They're counting on Corny leaving them a pile of money, but I wouldn't be surprised if he figured out a way to take it with him."

I guess we were all astonished that sweet old Mother Rose could turn so sour when it came to the Overtons.

The plans, she explained, were to hold the wake the following evening, Thursday, when the whole Overton family would turn out for a last look at Cornelius. The funeral would be Friday morning.

"Don't mind me if I seem short-tempered,"

Mother Rose continued, sipping her pale tea. "We're having a little bit of a crisis."

"What happened?"

"Our custodians just took off for Louisiana. Of all times! Ozzie Jackson does the outside—he takes care of the yard and the vehicles. And Maizie does the inside, dusting and so forth. They've worked for James for over twenty years, and this morning they upped and announced that they've got a sick grandchild over in Shreveport and away they went. James is beside himself."

This was the kind of challenge my mom loved. She said exactly what I knew she'd say: "Don't worry about a thing, Mother Rose. We'll take over for Ozzie and Maizie. Won't we, kids?"

"Uh-huh," I said.

"Sure."

"Yeah."

Mom got us organized. She and Robby would do the dusting and vacuuming. Steven volunteered to wax and polish Uncle James's Lincoln. (I could guess what my brother was thinking: If he did a good enough job, Uncle James might let him drive it.) And I went out to help Mr. Phillips with the yard work.

Stepping outside the air conditioning was a big shock. But there was Mr. Phillips, dressed as yesterday in black pants and a white shirt with black suspenders, weeding the flower beds. He straightened when he saw me and pushed his straw hat back on his head. "Morning," he said. Mr. Phillips had some gold on a front tooth that flashed when he smiled.

I explained that I was there to help pull weeds.

"Well now, isn't that real nice! You're called Emily Rose, that right?"

"Right."

He cocked his head and looked at me. "You sure you know the flowers from the weeds, young lady?"

I started naming them. "These are all petunias. Under the tree over there are impatiens and begonias. Those dark green things are hosta. The silvery green ones are dusty miller."

"Well, well, well! You must be related to Mother Rose! She is the best gardener in the neighborhood, you know that? Only in the last couple years, since her knees been bothering her, that she's not out here working right beside Ozzie Jackson. Every spring, along about April, she has me drive her to the nursery out on the Fort Worth highway and she goes up one row and down the next, saying, 'Let's have a dozen of this, Todd, and a dozen of that.' In the fall we go through the same thing again. She keeps the garden blooming all winter long. It's a gift she has."

While we pulled weeds and made sure there was plenty of mulch around the plants, Mr. Phillips asked me questions about where I went to school and what the weather was like in Connecticut and so forth. "Sure could use some of that around here," he said, when I told him about all the rain we'd had.

Sweat dripped off my nose. Mr. Phillips's shirt was damp, and once in a while he stopped to pull a handkerchief out of his pocket and wipe his face. "Guess y'all heard about the big funeral coming up here," he said.

I nodded. "Mr. Overton."

"Mr. *Cornelius* Overton," he said. "Guess Mother Rose has told you something about him."

"Sort of. I don't think she liked him much."

"Oh, those two have been taking digs at each other for ever so long."

"But why? She told us about his uncle who always sided with the white people. And his cousin Ella got Mother Rose and Catherine Jane Somebody in trouble. But that was seventy-five years ago! Have they been mad at each other for seventy-five years?"

Mr. Phillips gathered up some weeds and threw them in a basket. "Well, there's more to the story than she lets on. What she didn't tell you is that Mr. Cornelius Overton was so much in love with Rose Lee Jefferson he couldn't see right! All he could see was stars every time he looked at her! But she wouldn't give him a second look, no ma'am. For a long time she didn't look at *nobody* at all, kind of like her aunt Susannah, I think, who everybody thought was going to wind up an old maid. Susannah Jones was near thirty years old when she finally let Professor Prince talk her into marrying him! And your great-grandma kept saying all along she was never going to marry; she wanted to be *in-de-pen-dent*."

"But how do you know all this? You weren't even born yet, were you, Mr. Phillips?"

"I heard it from my momma, who was Mother Rose's girlhood friend. Stories get told over and over again, sometimes getting a little better, a little more exciting or interesting, than they were the first time around. Anyway, I heard some of these stories from my momma, and heard 'em again when they had the big golden anniversary party for Mother Rose and Pastor Ned.

"You know how they do at these things, people talk about their memories of the couple—things they recalled back when Ned Mobley was courting Rose Lee Jefferson. And my momma, who was still with us then, rest her soul, told how Rose Lee Jefferson had sworn an oath to her she was never going to marry. Now Ned was the nephew of the pastor of Forgiveness Church. He grew up over there in East Texas, and on the advice of his uncle went off and studied to be a preacher himself. When Pastor Mobley decided he was ready to retire—this was in about 1931, I b'lieve—here comes young Ned Mobley from over by Marshall and steps into the pulpit at Forgiveness in his uncle's place.

"Suddenly there isn't a girl in The Flats doesn't want to make him her husband! But first thing you know, this new preacher is keeping company with a Miss Rose Lee Jefferson, and isn't there quite a few young ladies upset by that, each thinking *she* is the one going to be Pastor Ned's wife and helpmeet! Now my momma didn't say so at the time, because that would not have been polite, but most upset of all was Cornelius Overton."

Mr. Phillips had a jar of cool water, and he found a scrap of shade for the two of us to take a rest. "How come he was so upset?" I asked. I was loving this story.

"Why, he'd been asking Rose Lee Jefferson to be his wife about once a month since she'd turned eighteen, and she'd been refusing him just as regular, citing this oath she'd taken never to marry. So he wasn't prepared for this turn of events. The Mobley-Jefferson wedding was something the whole town remembered and talked about. They were *still* talking about it the night of the golden anniversary."

Mr. Phillips adjusted his straw hat and picked up his rake. It looked as though our break was over. "I'll bet it was a nice party," I said.

"Oh my, yes, indeed. Just about everybody turned out at the church for the occasion. That was, let's see, about fifteen years ago. Mother Rose's two sisters, Lora Lee and Nancy Lee, were there—they'd been her bridesmaids, just young girls at the time of the wedding. Lots of food that evening, as you would expect, and even a big white wedding cake with a little bride and groom standing on top. The church put on the party, so everybody from Forgiveness Baptist was there, plus the AME church and that new one out on the highway, and even some white folks, like Mrs. Catherine Jane Plunkett and her son and daughter, that Mother Rose took care of long, long ago. I played the piano, any request that was called out. And that night, after it was over and everybody had gone home, we got the word—Pastor Ned gone to Glory, just like that."

"You mean he *died*? On their wedding anniversary?"

"That's right. One minute he's alive, the next minute he's crossed over. Must have been terrible for her—she's had so many losses, you know."

"Poor Mother Rose!"

This was just so sad! I hoped that somewhere Mother Rose had a wedding picture. I wanted to see her as a young bride, to know what my great-grandfather, Ned Mobley, looked like.

"But what about Cornelius Overton? Did he love her all that time?" I was beginning to feel a little sorry for the old guy in the coffin, too, no matter what Mother Rose said.

"That's what they say. He did marry eventually and had a son, Rosamond, nicknamed Rosie—now who you think he was named for? Rosie worked on the railroad and died in an accident some years back. Train run over him. Wasn't much left of him. Your uncle James did a pretty good job stitching him up so you couldn't hardly tell he'd been cut up so bad. The railroad paid his widow a nice sum of money, I think, and that's what set Rosie's son, Marcus, up so good, so's he can order the Monarch to put his granddaddy in. Plus, he makes pretty good money as a lawyer. Now he'll inherit Cornelius's money. It all adds up. Marcus Overton is bound to be the richest black man in Dillon."

WHEN EVERYTHING was ready, the inside of the funeral home spick-and-span and the garden beds weeded and pruned, Uncle James and Mr. Phillips wheeled the Monarch with Mr. Overton safely tucked inside into the slumber room. The lid was closed. I was getting used to the idea of being around a coffin, as long as I didn't think too much about the body that was in it.

A florist delivery truck arrived. Steven helped Mr. Phillips and the driver carry in the flowers, and Uncle James showed Mom how to arrange the baskets and vases around the casket. Uncle James himself placed the biggest basket right in front—two dozen red roses with a white satin ribbon draped across it and gold letters spelling GRANDFATHER.

"He sure is getting a lot of flowers," I said to Mr. Phillips when we had gone outside to give the brass work another shine.

Mr. Phillips rubbed a door hinge with his polishing rag. "Lots of folks afraid *not* to send flowers, in case Marcus Overton is keeping score." He stepped back to inspect his work and winked at me. "Or maybe in case Cornelius is."

TWELVE

Brandy

LIFE IS NEVER casual at a funeral home," Uncle James reminded us while we ate. Mom had volunteered to cook supper, omelettes as light and fluffy as clouds. "We must always be formal, always *punctilious*. Being raucous is out of place," he said, looking squarely at Robby. Robby looked squarely at his omelette. I didn't have to check *punctilious* or *raucous* in the dictionary to get the idea.

I was finding out that there are all kinds of rules to follow when you live in a funeral home—or just happen to be visiting, like us. You can't be noisy or run or slam doors or laugh out loud. That's because you might upset the people—"the bereaved," as Uncle James calls them—who come to see their loved ones laid out in the satin-lined coffins.

Also, nobody should be seen working at a funeral home. You must always be dressed up like you're going to church. Everything has to look perfect at all times. That was why the hearse and the van were parked in back when they were being washed and polished, and why even when he was pulling weeds, Mr. Phillips wore his black suit and white shirt and necktie. You never could tell when some bereaved person might appear and be upset by *normal*.

"Marcus and his sister will be stopping by in a little while," Uncle James announced, "to make sure everything is the way they want it."

"Huh!" Mother Rose snorted.

"Now, Mother Rose," Uncle James soothed. "They have a right, you know."

"I *know* they have a right! Doesn't make me like it, though."

"Best behavior, now," Uncle James warned.

We promised to do our best. Mother Rose just sniffed.

Steven and I helped Mom clean up the dishes, and then we were to get ready for the Wednesday night church service. Mother Rose and Uncle James had let us know that we were expected to go to church, too.

"What's this church like, Mom?" Steven asked.

"Well, if it's still the same as it was when I was little, there's lots of singing and praying, and the preacher gives a sermon, and then there's more praying and singing. I loved it when I was a child. Being in church was the best thing that happened all week. But it isn't like mass at all."

Our family is Catholic. Dad had been raised Catholic, but for a long time after they were married Mom didn't go to any church. Then when Robby was born, Mom decided to join the Catholic Church. Mom and Steven and Robby and I all got christened at the same time. Soon after that, Steven made his first communion. All three of us kids are altar servers, meaning we help the priest during mass. So it isn't like we don't know about church—we just didn't know about this *Baptist* kind of church.

Mother Rose had changed into a gray dress with black dots and a little gold pin with pearls in it. We expected that she'd probably want to show us off to everybody, and I was kind of nervous about the "only daughter of the only daughter of the only daughter" stuff. Before we left on our trip, Mom had bought me a couple of new outfits, which I needed anyway because I grew three inches last year. I planned to save the most sophisticated yellow-and-black one for the Juneteenth Jubilee. I put on the other outfit, a light blue jumper and a white shirt, and went outside to wait for the rest of the family.

I was sitting on the steps by the kitchen door, watching a giant bug make its way slowly across the cement walk, when a very tall girl with incredibly long legs like polished mahogany glided around the corner of the building. Masses of shiny black braids swung past her shoulders, and more braids were arranged on top of her head in kind of a crown. She looked like an African carving.

She didn't notice me at first. Her eyes were on Uncle James's Lincoln. She walked over to it and ran her hands lightly over the chrome. Steven had spent at least an hour polishing it, so I hoped she wasn't marking it up with fingerprints. Then she bent down and studied herself in the rearview mirror. She pulled a lipstick out of a tiny purse slung over her shoulder and dabbed some on her full lips. Next she examined her eye makeup. The mirror was small, and she had to crouch to check her amazing hair. I didn't move or make a sound, but she must have seen my reflection in the mirror. She whirled around and stared at me.

"Hi," I said.

"I thought everyone was inside," she said,

sounding suspicious. "I didn't know anybody was back here. That's my great-grandfather in there." She looked me up and down. "Cornelius Overton. He practically owned this part of town. Who are you? What are you doing here?"

"I'm visiting my great-grandmother, Mother Rose Mobley. She's lived here longer than anybody," I added.

The haughty princess with the royal braids stepped closer. "What's your name?"

"Emily Rose Chartier. What's yours?"

"Brandy Woodrow. Like Brandy, the singer. You know—Brandy Norwood, on TV? She is *so* great, isn't she? I love having the same name. It is so cool." While she talked, Brandy fooled with her loose braids, lifting them and letting them fall.

I said, "I'm named for my great-grandmother and my grandmother, who was named for my great-grandmother's art teacher. Talk about cool." It was like playing chess the way my father taught me. This was the opening gambit, and so far I was doing OK.

"Where do you live?" she demanded.

"Connecticut," I said. "Do you live in Dillon?"

She scowled. "I do now. I used to live in Dallas, which is way cooler than this hick town. But my momma moved us up here last winter, right in the middle of ninth grade. My dad's still in Dallas. He owns a car dealership, and his brother's a judge."

"Are they divorced?" I asked. "Your parents, I mean?"

"Yeah," she said, giving one of her braids a yank. "I still see him a lot, though." For about three seconds she sounded a touch less mocking, but then her mood switched again. "So what did you say your last name was?"

I repeated it, pouring on the French accent: *Shar-tee-YAY*. "It's French," I said. "My father is French American."

She hooted. "French American! My, *my*! And what do you think that makes *you*?"

"It makes me French American African American. I'm biracial. *Café au lait*," I said, feeling extremely sorry that I had let myself get into this. "Coffee with milk," I ended lamely. Bad move.

Brandy Woodrow gave me a look that would have peeled the bark off a tree. "And you think being a half-breed makes you one bit less black?" she asked scornfully, arching her perfect eyebrows.

That stung. I stood up and reached for the handle of the screen door. "No. It doesn't even mean I'm half black and half white. It means

I'm both. It means I'm *double*." I couldn't help my voice shaking.

"You might like to think you're half-and-half, but you're wrong," she said with a sneer. "Take a look in the mirror, girl, next time you get a chance. You think you're so good, 'cause you got those thin little French American lips and that French American hair that is *sooo* silky and wavy and nice. And that prissy white way of talkin'! Maybe up in Connecticut you can say you're double—whatever that means—and you can get away with telling that to those Yankees who believe just about anything. But around here you are *black*, Emily Rose. Black just like everybody else."

It wasn't a game anymore. I felt as though I'd been slapped. I grabbed the first thing I could think of to hit back at her. "Just because you've got the same first name as some famous star," I said, "that doesn't make *you* somebody great. All it makes you is mean!"

Brandy and I stared at each other. Then she tossed her headful of braids and strolled away on her unbelievably long legs. I rushed into the house, letting the screen door whoosh shut behind me, and raced for the bathroom, in danger of losing my supper.

THIRTEEN

Ned

ROSE LEE, *have you come to your senses yet? You ready to marry me?*

Mother Rose stared down at Cornelius Overton. He lay with his head propped on the ivory satin pillow, hands arranged on the satin coverlet. For once he had nothing to say. *Have you come to your senses yet?* is what he used to ask her every time he saw her. Death was what it took to shut him up.

Her momma had urged her to pay attention: *Rose Lee, he's well fixed. He'll take good care of you.* After the move out of Freedom, after Poppa gave up on the barbershop and went to work as a janitor at the Academy, things had never again gone the way they'd hoped. Until she finished high school, Rose Lee helped Momma with laundry. Hunched over the ironing board, pressing white ladies' linen sheets and embroidered napkins and delicate silk blouses, Rose Lee had dreamed of studying art, becoming an artist, like Miss Emily Firth. But she never dared speak of this foolish idea.

About the time Rose Lee was graduating from high school, Catherine Jane had come pleading: "Oh, please, please, Rose Lee, I don't know how to take care of this baby—she cries night and day and I am just beside myself! Do, *do* come help me, only until Phoebe sleeps through the night. You won't be asked to do another thing, I promise you. I'll pay you as much as Wilbur lets me . . ."

So she'd agreed. As Rose Lee suspected, Catherine Jane's banker husband wouldn't let her pay as much as both Catherine Jane and Rose Lee knew she deserved, but it was better than standing at the ironing board, the ache spreading between her shoulder blades. And tiny Phoebe, red-faced and howling in her bassinet draped with tulle, needed her.

The infant ceased her frantic crying as soon as Rose Lee picked her up and stroked the misery away. As Phoebe grew, she turned into a sparkling miniature of her mother, blond and blue-eyed, and willful. Phoebe loved Rose Lee, who returned the love, innocent and simple.

In a way Rose Lee loved Catherine Jane, too. *Liking* didn't begin to describe their bond—it was deeper than that—and complicated at times by Rose Lee's irritation and resentment of a spoiled, rich white woman's presumptions. If there was one thing Mrs. Eunice Bell had taught her daughter, it was bossing. Catherine Jane never let up.

Oh, Rose Lee, would you mind putting up this hem for me? I'm so clumsy with a needle, and I want to wear this new dress tonight. . . . Oh, Rose Lee, my geraniums are looking so peaked. Could you see if you can perk them up. . . . Oh, Rose Lee, Wilbur invited these men from the bank, and that Ella just falls apart if she has to do dinner for more than four people. Could you help her out, just this once? Please?

Ella Alexander, who had served Mrs. Eunice Bell, had been a wedding gift to Catherine Jane from her mother, who sent her over to help out the new bride. Rose Lee's aunt Tillie had taught the girl what she could about cooking and serving, even though Ella wasn't very bright. But it wasn't Ella's stupidity that was the problem—it was her cousin, Cornelius Overton, who sometimes came to fetch Ella home when she was done. And Cornelius would think up every which way he could to run into the nursemaid, Rose Lee Jefferson.

Each evening Rose Lee was to dress Phoebe in her nightie and take her down to her momma and poppa for a good-night kiss. Rose Lee didn't think much of Phoebe's poppa, the pompous Wilbur Plunkett. Wilbur was a friend of Edward Bell's, and although she had not a shred of proof, Rose Lee always believed that Wilbur was among the group of young men that tried to catch Henry to teach him a lesson for sassing Edward. Rose Lee wondered if Wilbur ever found out that his precious wife, Catherine Jane, behind the wheel of her poppa's Packard, was the reason they never caught Henry.

Then, as soon as Phoebe was asleep in her pretty little nursery, Rose Lee was free to leave —and hope that she could elude Ella's cousin. She never knew exactly when Cornelius would turn up. He was persistent. It seemed he wouldn't take no for an answer, and Rose Lee had given him plenty of *nos*.

Sometimes Rose Lee thought about quitting Catherine Jane's, but when she spoke of it Catherine Jane always persuaded her to stay. The little girl, Phoebe, was a dear child; that's what kept her there. Still, Rose Lee had made up her mind to leave anyway when Catherine Jane confided that she was expecting again.

"You can't leave me," Catherine Jane had wailed. "I don't know what I'd do without you,

Rose Lee! I'm positive Wilbur will let me pay you more."

"All right," Rose Lee sighed, even though she knew how tightfisted Wilbur Plunkett was.

If she was weak with Catherine Jane, Rose Lee was strong with Cornelius. He brought her gifts when he came back from his sales trips—lace hankies and boxes of peppermints and once a tiny gold rose hanging from a fine golden chain. "For the only Rose in my life," he'd written on a small white card enclosed in the box. "Marry me."

"I will never marry. Never," she told him, handing back the necklace.

"That's what you're saying today," he said with a grim smile.

"What I say every day," she retorted.

The next month he was back again, another present, another proposal, another refusal. This went on for four years.

On Juneteenth 1931 Rose Lee's people observed the tenth anniversary of the end of Freedomtown. Those who had hauled their homes out to The Flats had been joined in the intervening years by new families moving to town. The newcomers built houses and planted trees and flowers and put in vegetable gardens. The city had finally finished the Negro school, named W. E. B. Du Bois, in honor of the cofounder of the National Association for the Advancement of Colored People, to replace the school that burned down. The members of Forgiveness Baptist Church had raised the money to build a new church. After ten years even the old-timers had to admit that The Flats wasn't such a bad place to live after all, although still every bit as dusty and muddy as Freedom had ever been.

It was during that Juneteenth tenth anniversary service that Pastor Mobley called for his nephew, Ned Mobley, to step forward. This, Pastor Mobley announced, was his successor.

After the service as they spread their Juneteenth picnic in the church grove, Ned stopped by to speak to Rose Lee and her family. His smile was as white as his crisp linen suit, as gleaming as his silk tie. He had kind eyes. She looked at him and liked what she saw. A week later he came to call on her. They sat on the porch and talked. She listened to him and liked what she heard. He asked her to walk with him at the Fourth of July celebration.

But Catherine Jane had planned a big Independence Day party in her backyard, and naturally she expected Rose Lee to help out. "I'm sorry, but I can't," Rose Lee explained to Catherine Jane. "I have other plans." There followed the usual pleading and wheedling that almost always broke down Rose Lee's objections. This time Rose Lee stood firm.

Ned and Rose Lee did not stay long at the celebration, which featured a fish fry and homemade peach ice cream. Instead, they began to walk, not paying attention to where they were going. They walked far out into the country. Everything was happening before Rose Lee even understood that *anything* was happening. They had known each other two weeks. She felt lightheaded, short of breath. They stopped to rest.

Ned commenced a long-winded speech—begging her to search her heart to discern her true feelings, to pray over what he was about to ask, to take as much time as she needed before answering—

"The answer's *yes*," Rose Lee said, not giving him a chance to ask his question. "I'll marry you."

He'd kissed her fingers, one by one. "When?" he asked.

"Soon as I can sew a dress," she answered, and flung her arms around his neck.

The wedding was planned for September. Grandmother Lila helped Rose Lee make a shimmering white satin wedding gown trimmed with ivory lace. Rose Lee's younger sisters sewed dresses of lavender dotted swiss. Cooking started in every kitchen in The Flats a week in advance.

There hadn't been a wedding like this in the Jefferson family, or in The Flats, for a long time—Aunt Susannah and Professor Prince had just disappeared one weekend and come back married.

The only sour note was Cornelius Overton. He had even tried to convince his uncle, Gus Alexander, to block the congregation's approval of Ned Mobley as its new pastor. Usually Gus was wishy-washy, but this time he stiffened his spine. "There are other girls as pretty as Rose Lee Jefferson," he reportedly advised his heart-broken nephew, "and a whole lot easier to get along with."

"I won't forget this, Rose Lee," Corny warned her a few days before the wedding. "I loved you; I was faithful to you; I would have waited as long as you asked me to."

"I made you no promises, Corny," she reminded him. "I told you, I believe, I had no intention to marry."

"That was plainly a lie."

"What I meant, Corny, but was too kind to say to you, was that I had no intention to marry *you*." She'd tried to walk away from him, but he grabbed her wrist.

"Bad things gonna happen to you, Rose Lee," he'd said. "I feel it. This is the wrong thing for you to do. That man isn't worth your little finger. That phony smile of his! I'd be worried if I was you. He might be telling you he loves you, but I hear he says that quite a bit, to other girls. I travel around a lot, you know, and I've heard things, Rose Lee!"

"Stop it, Corny," she warned him. "You don't know what you're talking about."

"Bad things gonna happen, Rose Lee. Mark my words."

It was like a curse he'd laid on her. She remembered it when they lowered John Henry's tiny coffin into the muddy ground not six months after he was born. She remembered it again as she sat by Charley's bedside and watched him leave her, breath by breath. She remembered it standing by Emily's grave, and she'd thought of it for the last time as she'd rocked Ned's lifeless body in her arms.

Now Mother Rose gazed down at Cornelius Overton's wrinkled brown face, lips forever sealed. *Bad things happen, Cornelius. They happen to everybody, even without you wishing them.*

When she glanced up, Marcus Overton was tucking his white silk handkerchief into the breast pocket of his suit coat. He stared at her across the open coffin, his mouth set in a hard line.

FOURTEEN

Forgiveness Baptist

MOTHER ROSE led us to the front of the church and lined us up in the second pew—Uncle James on the end, then Steven and Robby and Mom and then me, right next to Mother Rose, who sat on the aisle. As Mom promised, there was lots of singing. Mr. Phillips, still dressed in his black suit, was playing the piano in a jazzy style that made your feet tap all on their own, and the choir sang a couple of anthems with everybody clapping. It was just a small church, not even half as big as St. Brigid's, but the singing was *loud*.

I was still pretty shaky from my encounter with Brandy Woodrow, and I certainly hadn't expected to end up sitting practically eyeball to eyeball with her. She stood in the third row of the choir facing us. She looked straight at me and then let her eyes slide away, as though she hadn't even seen me or didn't want to be bothered. I was furious. *The first kid I meet in Dillon,* I thought, *and she turns out to be totally hateful. So what if her parents got divorced and she thinks Dillon is for hicks?* I resolved not to look at her again.

Pastor Hilton, who is shiny black and has a beautiful, lilting accent, preached a long sermon. "He's from Jamaica," Mother Rose whispered. The sermon was about the burning of black churches and how we must help the brothers and sisters in Greenville to rebuild and how we need to be watchful even here in Dillon.

"Amen," boomed a solemn voice from the back, and several others echoed, "Amen. Yes, amen."

Then came a string of announcements. The people in charge of the Juneteenth Diamond Jubilee had big ideas, since this was a once-in-a-lifetime event. The Jubilee would run for five nights, starting Saturday with a reunion banquet and dance at the Dillon Inn for alumni of W. E. B. Du Bois School.

Uncle James was chairman of the banquet committee. He got to his feet and reminded the congregation that everybody was invited who had attended the old "colored school." A good turnout was expected, but a few tickets were still available.

"Now don't be having so much fun on Saturday night," the pastor teased, wagging his finger, "that you forget to come here Sunday morning!" The main preacher would be Freedom Gibbons, the first baby born after the move from Freedomtown to The Flats and also among the first to leave Dillon with his parents after the move. "Pastor Gibbons is a retired preacher in Kansas City, and I promise you he can be counted upon to give us a fiery sermon."

Mother Rose whispered loudly in my ear, "Freedom's my cousin Cora's boy."

After Sunday church, the pastor continued, there'd be a mass march to Martin Luther King Jr. Park over by the new elementary school for a big, old-fashioned picnic. The chairwoman, a robust woman with coppery hair and a wide gap between her front teeth, announced from her seat in the choir that the catering committee had consulted Mother Rose in order to come up with an authentic Freedomtown Juneteenth menu.

"Mother Rose can remember just exactly how her momma fried the chickens and baked the peach cobblers, and what all kind of biscuits and cakes her aunties and her friends' mommas fixed back then. Nobody going to go away hungry, that I promise."

Pastor Hilton continued with the schedule. Monday night a teacher from the community college would give a talk entitled "Perspectives of Freedomtown, 1870–1921." Tuesday night each church was planning something different. The star attraction would be Mother Rose, the oldest living member of Forgiveness Baptist and the only one who actually remembered the move from Freedom.

Wednesday night, June nineteenth, the final event of the Jubilee celebration would be held at the Great Hall of Dillon Community College. Church choirs were scheduled to sing, a children's group had been practicing some dances, and after a few short speeches, everybody was invited to partake of refreshments.

It took so long to get through all those announcements that Robby was falling asleep against Mom's shoulder. But the congregation was anything but tired. They were definitely wired, and they needed a hymn and an anthem from the choir before they could settle down and get on with the next thing: the passing of Cornelius Overton.

Pastor Hilton offered expressions of sympathy to the bereaved family. A broad-shouldered man in the first pew on the left stood up, dabbed at his eyes with a handkerchief, which he then tucked neatly back into his pocket, and bowed his head.

"Marcus," Mother Rose hissed at me.

"Words cannot begin to express our feelings of sorrow for the loss of this great and loving man," Marcus said after a sober silence. "I know the whole community shares our belief that this was indeed a giant among men, and yet a humble servant of God."

Mother Rose shifted around on the pew beside me, twisting her gnarled old hands in her lap. The pastor called for another hymn, a quiet one this time.

Then, at the very end, Pastor Hilton said, "I believe our beloved Mother Rose is blessed to have some family with her this evening." He beamed down at us. "I wish to call upon her at this time to introduce her loved ones to our community."

Mother Rose had us stand up one by one and turn around to face the congregation. First she introduced Mom as "Susan, the only daughter of my only daughter, Emily." That got some nice applause. Then it was my turn. "Emily Rose," she said, caressing each syllable the way she did, "only daughter of the only daughter of my only daughter." There was more applause and a woman called out, "Yes! Praise Jesus!" I couldn't see Brandy without turning around, which was a shame. I would love to have seen her face.

Robby was next. Robby looks more French American than African American, more Chartier than Pratt. He doesn't have to do much explaining to people about being double, because everybody just assumes he's white. He popped up fast, grinned, and sat down faster. *Clap clap clap.* "Thank you, Lord!" someone said.

Then Mother Rose got to Steven. Steven is almost as dark as Mom. He is also tall and devastatingly handsome—my friends all say that he looks like Denzel Washington, and at least three of them are secretly in love with him, even though he has a girlfriend, Samantha Chu. Brandy, whom I faced again, practically fell out of her choir seat, giving Steven a *look* that was disgustingly worshipful. I glared her a fierce message: *Don't even think of it, Brandy Woodrow.*

"This young man is a smart fellow," Mother Rose was saying. "Yesterday I was with my family, here all the way from Connecticut for our Juneteenth Jubilee, and my cousin James kindly consented to take us on a drive around Old Freedom and other places of interest. We passed by the old Ragsdale house, where my aunt Susannah Jones and her husband, Professor

Horace Prince, once made their home, and where James was born."

Uncle James massaged his forehead with the tips of his fingers.

"Now you all know what terrible shape that pretty old house has fallen into, over there on Williams Street," Mother Rose continued. "And this young man here, my great-grandson, said, 'Mother Rose, why don't you move that house? Why don't you just pick it up and put it back where it belongs?' he said. 'And fix it back up the way it was?' "

I didn't remember that Steven had said all that. Steven ducked his head, staring at the floor. "Seems to me," Mother Rose continued, "that this is divine inspiration—God Himself telling us to take that old house, that last remaining piece of Freedomtown, and to move it back home where it belongs."

Mother Rose paused and looked around, like she expected everybody to stand up right then and go get the Ragsdale house and haul it over to Center Park. Steven kind of folded down into his seat, waiting for his divine inspiration to end.

" 'Home'?" Pastor Hilton asked, leaning on the pulpit and raising his voice above the buzz in the congregation. "Where do you mean by 'home,' Mother Rose?"

"I mean, back to old Freedomtown, of course. Not the exact spot—the old folks center is there. But back to the park where Freedom used to be."

The pastor smiled the way you would at a child who has just come up with a cute but totally impractical idea. "That's a fine suggestion, Mother Rose," he said in a patronizing tone. "Something we may all want to consider. Now let's join in singing hymn number two hundred and seventy-three, 'Blest Be the Tie.' " Mr. Phillips hesitated, but Pastor Hilton nodded vigorously in his direction, and he began to play.

When the service ended, many people stayed behind to say hello to Mom and us kids. A lot of the older ones hugged her and said they hadn't seen her since she was just a little thing and how happy they were that she had come back for the Jubilee. "And you brought these lovely children with you," they said, giving us a thorough looking over.

I lost track of Brandy Woodrow during the commotion, but I had a feeling she hadn't lost track of me—and *especially* not of Denzel Washington Chartier.

FIFTEEN

Special World

"AND WAS Mr. Marcus Overton pleased with how Corny looks?" Mother Rose asked. She sliced a third of a banana over a handful of cornflakes and passed the rest of the banana to Uncle James.

"Seemed to be," Uncle James said mildly, adding the banana to his bowl.

"I will never forget the fuss Marcus put up when we did his grandma," Mother Rose said. "That was Corny's wife, Mildred, poor soul! Marcus didn't like the way her hair looked, somehow, and the skin tone wasn't the way he thought it ought to be. I just wanted to shake him and say, 'She's dead, Marcus, that's why she looks that way!' But naturally you can't do a thing like that."

After breakfast I found a broom and went out to sweep the steps and the sidewalk. Mr. Phillips steered the lawn mower back and forth as carefully as if he were shaving his chin. More flowers arrived for Mr. Overton. By early afternoon everything was ready.

The wake was scheduled for seven o'clock that evening. Mom decided that we would all go to the slumber room together to pay our respects and shake hands with Marcus and his sister and the other relatives. "Just say you're sorry about their loss." Then we would pause briefly by the casket and think a kind thought about Cornelius Overton. After that we could leave.

As the afternoon wore on Steven was getting restless. Finally he said to Mom, "I think I'll walk over to those tennis courts in Center Park and hit a few balls." Steven is a very good tennis player. He's on the high school tennis team.

"Sure, why not? Have fun," Mom said. "Just be back in time to be showered and dressed before dinner. We'll be eating early. The wake, you know."

"I never thought," Mother Rose said, watching Steven bound out the door, "when I was a twelve-year-old girl, that someday my great-grandson would be playing tennis in the Garden of Eden." I remembered then that the tennis courts were in the exact spot where her grandpa had had his beautiful garden. "I think Grandfather Jim might like that."

Later a round-faced boy, who turned out to be Mr. Phillips's grandson, Nathan, showed up and invited Robby to come to his house in the next block to see his tropical fish. Then Mom announced that she was going to buy groceries, since keeping up with our appetites can be a challenge.

"Want to come with me, Emmy?" she asked. "Uncle James is lending me his car."

On the one hand I was thinking how much fun it could be to taunt my brothers that I'd been riding around in the Lincoln. On the other hand, I really hate grocery shopping.

"If you'd care to stay here, I'd be glad for your company, Emily Rose," Mother Rose said, and that settled it.

She was sipping another cup of tea. I poured myself a tall glass of iced tea from the giant jug Uncle James keeps in the refrigerator. "Why don't you come on back to my little room and bring your tea with you," Mother Rose said. "I have some things I want to show you."

I followed Mother Rose to her room, pleased with the idea of having her all to myself. I loved her stories about growing up in Freedomtown and helping Grandfather Jim in Mrs. Eunice Bell's garden as well as in his Garden of Eden, and how his white lilac became a symbol of everything that had happened to the community. I wanted to hear more.

But the minute I entered her room, I caught my breath. In most ways it was almost exactly the kind of bedroom you'd expect an old lady to have: blue-flowered wallpaper, a wooden bed with a crocheted spread, a velvet-covered chair with most of the fuzz rubbed off the velvet. But there was one big difference: All four walls were covered with paintings.

It was like I had just stepped through a secret door into a special world. I stood there staring, probably with my mouth open. Most of the paintings were about the size of a newspaper page, although there were a couple of larger ones and a few smaller ones. In some pictures there was a whole crowd; in others only one or two people, but they were all scenes of people busy *doing* things. The artist had taken ordinary moments in their daily lives and changed them into something beautiful.

"Who painted all these pictures?" I managed to ask.

"I did," Mother Rose said.

"*You* did? I didn't know—," I began, and then I just shut up and looked.

My eyes jumped from one painting to another

and finally settled on one hanging above the old-fashioned dresser. It was a portrait of a tall black woman in a bright red dress. She wore red shoes and a slouchy little red hat, and she was carrying a red umbrella. She was as stately as a queen.

"Now that's Aunt Susannah," Mother Rose said. "James's mother. It's how I remember her best, when she came to visit from St. Louis. She wore that outfit for Juneteenth and set some tongues to wagging, I can tell you. My momma's included. How I did love her red parasol!"

"I didn't know you could paint," I said, which might take the prize for the year's most stupid remark. But I could hardly get it through my head that Mother Rose had done all this.

She settled herself on the edge of the bed. "Well, I always did like to draw, you know, and I even dreamed of being an artist someday. But I had to work, and then I got busy with a husband and children," she went on, "and there was no time for art. For years I never even picked up a pencil. But nineteen thirty-four was such a hard year I had to do *something*." She shook her head sadly.

"My second baby, John Henry, was scarcely in the ground when word came that my brother had been killed in some kind of accident. Next my poppa died. That was just about the last straw for my momma. A great darkness descended upon us. And somehow, the only way I could work my way out of the darkness was to make pictures. I decided to try to paint. I wanted the color, do you see? So I wrote to Miss Emily Firth in Philadelphia—we had kept in touch over the years—and asked her if there was a book I could read that would show me what to do. She wrote back, 'Don't read anything—just paint.' She sent me a few partly used tubes of paint and some rather worn brushes. That was the Depression, you know, and Miss Emily had lost her teaching job and had no more money to spare for art supplies than I did. But she sent me what she could. Why, child, I had scarcely enough money to put food on the table, we were so poor.

"I was the preacher's wife and expected to help out with the church, but I had to find other work, too. During the week Ned went over to East Texas to pick cotton with his brothers, then came back here Saturday night. Catherine Jane's husband's bank closed, and she couldn't pay me to come every day. So I'd go to her once a week and do her cleaning and laundry and some of the cooking, too, all in that one day, and then another day I'd go to her sister-in-law's and help out there, too. So we got by.

"You know what I did?" she said with a chuckle. "I put my spare pennies and once in a good while an extra nickel in a jar I kept hidden, and when I'd saved enough I'd buy me a tube of oil paint or a piece of canvas. If I didn't have money for regular artist's paint, I used house paint. If I couldn't afford a linen canvas, I used an old piece of wood, or even a hunk of cardboard. But I kept on at it. I painted our life. And there it is," she said, "hanging on the walls."

"But when did you have time to do this, Mother Rose?"

"Late at night, mostly. After everybody else was asleep, I'd get out of bed and slip back to the kitchen and paint. We survived the Depression, then we had the war. Not everybody survived that." She pointed to a figure in a tan uniform in the midst of a picnic. "That's Reuben Prince, Aunt Susannah's older boy, at the Fourth of July fish fry, last time he was home on leave. The little fellow looking up at him and saluting? That's Uncle James."

Near Mother Rose's bed was a picture of a man in a barber chair, having his hair cut. A row of black men in work clothes sat waiting their turn, lined up against a yellowish wall. A little girl peeked around the edge of a green curtain at the far end of the room.

"That one's Pastor Mobley, the *first* Pastor Mobley, in the chair, getting an edge, as they called it," Mother Rose explained. "And on the end, next in line, is Mr. Morgan, the undertaker. He was the father of my best friend, Bessie. Then next to him is Mr. Ross, who was head janitor over at the white girls' school, and beside him is Mr. Webster, who ran the Sun-Up Café. I bet your momma's Café au Lait is a whole lot different from the Sun-Up!"

"Who's the girl peeking around the curtain?" I asked, even though I could guess.

"Why that's Rose Lee Jefferson, sticking her nose in where it doesn't belong!" She burst out laughing, enjoying her joke.

One wall of Mother Rose's bedroom was mostly memories of Freedomtown: Grandmother Lila rocking a baby in the midst of a sea of little kids. Grandfather Jim hoeing a garden, almost buried in white and purple flowers. Her friends Bessie and Lou Ann carrying suitcases, in front of a railroad car marked COLORED ONLY. A woman bent over a washtub with a clothesline full of stiff white sheets like sails on a ship behind her. "It made Momma real mad that I painted her like that," Mother Rose explained. "She wanted me to paint her in her church clothes."

I loved the picture Mother Rose had painted

of her wedding. It was like you're standing in the pastor's place. The bride and groom gaze at you solemnly, and behind them are rows and rows of church pews filled with men dressed up in white shirts and neckties and women in flowered hats. The same little girl from the barbershop sits in the second row, and she's smiling—Rose Lee, present at her own future wedding.

Most of the pictures glowed with color, but one of the big canvases was all black and white and shades of gray: a long procession of mourners carrying three black coffins to a lonely cemetery with bare black trees and stark white tombstones. In the gray sky above them, pale doves held black roses in their beaks. "That's a funeral for all three of my children," she explained. "I put them all in one painting. My pictures aren't what you call realistic. They're not meant to be like photographs. They're recollections. That way, I'm not always worrying about whether somebody's nose is just right or if a certain tree grew this way or that."

I noticed a canvas on the floor, propped against the wall and turned so that I couldn't see what was on it. "Is that another painting?" I asked.

Mother Rose nodded. "Take a look," she said.

It was a young man formally dressed in an old-fashioned suit with pinstriped pants, standing stiffly with his arms at his sides. In the middle of his body was a heart-shaped hole. His round white eyes with black pupils stared blankly out of the painting. "Who is it, Mother Rose?"

"Cornelius Overton," she said. "Seventy years ago, give or take."

I sighed. "Mother Rose," I said carefully, "I know it's none of my business, but why do you hate Mr. Overton so much?"

"I don't *hate* him, Emily Rose. That wouldn't be Christian. I just can't *stand* him!" she said fiercely. "Haven't been able to abide the man for seventy years, you know what I'm saying?"

And just when I thought I might hear another chapter about Mother Rose and Mr. Overton, the back door opened and closed and I heard Mom ask in a quiet, funeral-home voice, "Anybody home?"

"May I show Mom?" I whispered to Mother Rose.

"Anytime you want to show your momma, you can. Now it's your secret to share."

But as I ran out to help Mom carry in the groceries, I made a selfish decision: I wanted the secret of Mother Rose's special world to belong only to me for a little while longer.

SIXTEEN

Marissa

HEY, WHAT'S UP?" I asked Steven as he raced past me up the stairs.

"Gotta get showered and changed," he called over his shoulder. "I met some people. Catch you later, Em."

"You got a letter from Samantha," I hollered after him, and then remembered about not hollering.

He stopped in midflight. "I did?" He turned around and came back downstairs slowly. He didn't look as thrilled as I thought he would. "Where is it?"

"I put it on your dresser."

Steven's girlfriend back in Northdale was obviously pining for him in a big way. The letter that had come with Uncle James's mail was thick, probably several pages, and definitely Samantha Chu's handwriting, all smooth ovals, as if she had been practicing penmanship. I also had mail, a postcard from Boston with a picture of Faneuil Hall, "The Cradle of Liberty." "The swan boats are *interesting,*" Alicia had written, code for *boring*.

I like Samantha—she doesn't like to be called Sam—who is a champion gymnast. She has a small, compact body and wears her shiny black hair cut in thick bangs almost to her eyebrows. Samantha, who is very serious about everything, including my brother, intends to be an astronomer.

It's hard to tell what Steven is serious about, besides having a good time. He intends to run a successful company someday. Sometimes he talks about being an actor, and he belongs to the drama club at his high school. He goes around the house spouting lines from Shakespeare, like "I kissed thee ere I killed thee. No way but this: killing myself, to die upon a kiss," from *Othello*. Actually he's pretty good, and he does get major parts in most of the school plays. But he isn't sure he'd be able to support himself as an actor, so he plans to get a degree in business administration, too.

"Left brain versus right brain," Dad says. "A good way to drive yourself crazy." Mom just shrugs. "Do whatever's going to make you happy" is her advice, to which Steven always replies, "But I don't know what that *is*." Meanwhile, he plays a lot of tennis and hangs out with Samantha. Or he did before we left Connecticut.

Naturally I was curious about who it was he'd met. My intuition told me it was a female. Steven does not generally grin goofily when he makes plans to get together with one of his guy friends. But I have learned that the best way to handle Steven is to keep quiet and wait for him to tell me.

My intuition was confirmed when Steven came downstairs later dressed in his girl-impressing clothes, a blue-and-white-checked shirt and white jeans. "So what's happening?" I asked fake-casually, as though I hadn't already figured out part of it.

"I'm going out with some people I met at the tennis court."

"Umm. What's her name?"

"Marissa," he said, giving me a you-think-you're-so-smart look. "Marissa Plunkett. You should see her play tennis, Emmy! Fantastic serve. Stupendous backhand."

Fantastic. *Stupendous*. He does sometimes exaggerate. "And you met her at the city courts?"

"Basically, yes. See, I was just fooling around, slamming a few against the backboard, not even smashing hard because it was so frigging *hot*. And these girls came out of the library, which is on the other side of the parking lot, except the only shade is over by the courts where they had parked this cherry red BMW convertible. So they stopped to watch, and we started talking—you know, what's your name, where're you from. And then this girl, Marissa, asks me if I want to come out to her club and play. That it's got much better courts—clay, not asphalt—and since I'm from out of town she can get me in as her guest."

Mom, who was in the kitchen making avocado soup, leaned in the doorway. "Club?" she asked. "As in, *country* club?"

"Right. So we get in her car, the BMW, and we drive out to the Dillon Golf and Tennis Club. She signs me in at the front gate. The other girls decide to go to the pool for a swim, but Marissa and I start playing on this primo court. And she almost beats me, because she's acclimated to this sweltering heat and humidity, and I'm just about ready to collapse. Not only that, but she's got this killer serve. And she'll go for just about any shot, no matter how ridiculous. She makes a lot of them, too."

"I take it she's white," Mom said.

"A blond, blue-eyed Texan," Steven said coolly.

"Uh-*huh*," Mom murmured.

Steven shrugged and went on with his story. "So then we sat on the patio and ordered Cokes and chips and some kind of salsa that almost burned my tongue right out of my mouth. She wouldn't let me pay for any of it, because she signed for it and the bill goes to her father. 'Next time, bring your suit,' she said, 'and we'll go for a swim after.' And then she drove me back here."

"So what are your plans now?" Mom asked.

"I don't know exactly. Marissa wants to show me around town, and then we might stop at a barbecue place she knows. Marissa says Texas barbecue is an experience. So I won't be back for dinner. Mom, I don't have to be here for the wake, do I?"

"No, I guess not. You don't know the Overtons, and I don't believe anyone would take it wrong if you went out and had some fun. Just be careful, OK?" She sounded worried, as though Marissa might kidnap him or something. And I was pretty annoyed, because how come he didn't have to go to Corny's wake and I did?

"Sure," he said, giving her a hug. "You know me, always look both ways before I cross the street."

She ducked away. "No, I'm serious, Steven. You're in the South. Marissa's white. Be *aware*, that's all I'm saying."

I asked evilly, "What did Samantha have to say? How's everything back in Connecticut?"

I was glad to see him get a guilty look. "I haven't read her letter yet," he said. "I'll read it later, when I get back." He smooched Mom loudly on the cheek, patted me on the head, which he knows makes me crazy, and was out the back door and gone.

"Steven met some young people over at the tennis court," Mom explained later to Uncle James and Mother Rose, when we sat down to eat Mom's avocado soup. "One of the girls offered to show him around and then have some barbecue, he said."

Mother Rose nodded. "That's nice," she said. "It's good for young people to get out and do things together. I worry so what's happening to our young folks today. The drug problem, all the violence, everyone with guns."

"Do you know with whom he was going?" Uncle James asked in his formal way. He'd told us that his father, Professor Prince, taught Latin at W. E. B. Du Bois—Latin!—and insisted on proper grammar.

"I didn't catch the name," she said. "I have to trust his judgment."

"Marissa Plunkett," I said. I wished Steven hadn't gone off with the white girl and her friends. It wasn't just that I thought he should be true to Samantha. But here was Mom warning him to be careful because he was going with white people.

Uncle James and Mother Rose looked at each other. "Marissa Plunkett? Wouldn't that be . . . ?" Mother Rose trailed off.

"Dr. Harold Plunkett's daughter," Uncle James finished.

"What?" Mom asked.

Uncle James translated. "It's possible, likely even, that Steven's new friend is the granddaughter of Tom Plunkett, whom Mother Rose cared for as a small child."

Mother Rose began explaining who was who—that this Tom Plunkett was Catherine Jane's spoiled son. "Racist through and through," she said. "Just an old-time white supremacist. You couldn't get much worse than Tom Plunkett on that. Susan, your momma had her run-ins with Tom back when they were integrating the schools." Mother Rose appeared to have finished with her soup after three spoonfuls.

"She did? What kind of run-ins did she have?" Mom asked.

"It's a long story, child," Mother Rose said, "and not a very happy one."

"I question the girl's motives in inviting Steven into this situation," Uncle James said sharply. "Somebody needs to tell that young man to watch his back." He checked his watch and stood up. "Now if you will excuse me," he said. "I do hate to leave you with the cleanup, but the wake begins in a half hour and I expect Marcus here at any moment."

Mom waved him away. "Don't worry, Uncle James, we'll take care of it." But her attention was fixed on Mother Rose. "Tell me the story!" she begged. "Please!"

SEVENTEEN

Tom Plunkett

INSIDE MY HEAD, Mother Rose thought, *it's like some old boardinghouse—lots of little rooms, each one with a door that's shut tight until you need to go in there and find something that matters.*

Susan and Emily Rose, connected to her by that long chain of birthing but pulled so far from her by circumstance, watched her with their wide, bright eyes. They were waiting for her to open the door to one of those little rooms in her memory. She turned a knob and saw Tom Plunkett, heavyset, red-faced, rich, powerful. At the same time she saw the sullen little boy who used to sass her. She saw also the arrogant young man who never bothered to thank her for the graduation gift she'd sent, a brass paperweight in the shape of Texas.

Tom Plunkett, member of the school board representing the wealthy Fourth District, believed separate but equal was just fine, and separate but unequal wasn't a bad idea, either—it kept the Negroes in their place. The Supreme Court said otherwise and ordered schools to desegregate. In Dillon black people with children in the lower grades were given "freedom of choice": They could send their kids clear across town to Robert E. Lee Elementary or keep them in their own colored school.

Mother Rose could hear her daughter Emily's worried voice thirty-some years ago, when schools were starting to be integrated. "Momma, I don't know what to do. Susan's so young. I'm afraid of what might happen to her." Rose Lee Jefferson Mobley had said, "Don't worry, I'll take her. And sit with her all day, if need be."

"You remember me walking you to school every day?" Mother Rose asked Susan now.

Susan leaned toward her intently with Emily's same look of fierce concentration. Then slowly the memory lit her face. "Yes, I do remember! I carried my lunch in a little metal box with a schoolhouse painted on it. And now I remember how scared I was! I had never been around white kids before, and they all stared at us—

there were only two or three of us, isn't that right? I was so glad you'd be waiting outside to pick me up when school let out in the afternoon! But now that I think about it, I don't know why it was *you* who took me and not Momma."

"Because your momma was busy teaching over at W. E. B. Du Bois. That was before they closed it. Professor Adams, the principal then—he took over from Professor Prince—he had her teaching home economics and geography, and supervising the drama club and the glee club on the side. Your momma could teach anything! She was a brilliant student, you know. She went through four years of college in only three years with straight A's. Hardly any black girls went to college back then. It was a Negro college, of course, because back in the fifties black students were not allowed to attend white schools.

"She was teaching something in all ten grades. See, at first they took just the eleventh and twelfth grades from W. E. B. Du Bois over to Dillon High School—it was to be done in stages. Your grandpa organized the transportation for our boys and girls to go over there. For the younger children, it was up to the parents if they wanted to send them to the white school or not. So I offered to take you across town to Robert E. Lee. Do you remember that for a few weeks I stayed right there with you, to make sure you'd be all right? I worried so about you!"

"But why?" asked Emily Rose. "Why didn't you want Mom to go to W. E. B. Du Bois if her mother was even teaching there?"

"Because we wanted the best education for your momma, even if that meant hardship. Much as we all loved W. E. B. Du Bois, and it was dear to our hearts because we waited so long to get it after the old one burned, we knew it wasn't near good enough—not for your momma, not for any of our children. Worn-out books, no library in the school and we couldn't use the public one—even though it was built right on the site of our old Knights of Pythias Hall! No equipment to teach physics or chemistry, some old maps left over from before the war, football uniforms sent over by the white school, all faded and raggedy by the time they got to our boys. People said it didn't matter, a uniform was a uniform, but it mattered to our boys, sure it did! Lots of heart at W. E. B. Du Bois, truly, but it also takes enough books and paper and pencils to go around. We wanted them to make it good as the white schools, and let white children come there, too. But no use telling that to Tom Plunkett. He proposed to shut down the Negro school, and the white school board agreed. It was a slap in the face to the whole Negro community when whites refused to send their children there."

Old as I am, Mother Rose thought, *eighty-seven years now, going on eighty-eight, and I still get so damn mad at that old so-and-so I can't see straight.*

"Mother Rose," Susan said carefully. *She is such a careful girl, much more careful than her momma was*, Mother Rose thought, and nodded, waiting for her question. "Given that Tom Plunkett is a racist and a white supremacist, do you think Steven's friendship with his granddaughter, this Marissa Plunkett, poses any kind of a problem?"

Mother Rose pondered how to answer. "I know her daddy, too, Dr. Harold Plunkett. He's a heart doctor. He wants to put a pacemaker in my chest. I'm considering it. Not a bad man, so far as I know. But *white*, Susan! *White!* Folks around here don't go much for mixing, you know. White *or* black, they don't like it. Because we don't trust each other."

"Don't you trust white people?" Emily Rose asked tremulously. "My dad is white, so I am, too, partly," she added in a rush, sounding like she might commence crying.

"I know that, sweet child." Mother Rose searched for the right thing to say. "Everybody's different," she said, the best she could think of under the circumstances. And the circumstances made her uneasy.

PECULIAR HOW CHILDREN from the same family can turn out so different. She had cared for Tommy Plunkett and his sister, Phoebe, almost as though they were her own dear children. And those two had grown up as different from each other as though they were from separate families, one family good and kind and servants of God, the other nasty and selfish.

Phoebe had been an angel, and she'd remained a kind of angel all her life. Phoebe was married to Pete Kingsley, a builder. It was Phoebe who got Mother Rose and then Emily to join the Christian Women's Action Group back in the sixties, when there was all the fuss about integration. Phoebe had come to visit Mother Rose and explained it: "At first we're just going to get together at a different house each month for coffee."

Mother Rose had sniffed at that notion. "Is this Christian *white* women or Christian *black* women you're talking about?"

"Both," Phoebe said. "Equal numbers is what we're trying for. Then we're planning to go out for lunch together, or maybe just a lemonade or something. To support restaurant owners who treat black customers well. And also, so folks can see black women and white women together just being *friends*."

"All right," Mother Rose had agreed, smiling to cover her misgivings. "I'll join."

When it was Emily's turn to have the group gather at her house she was nervous, embarrassed to have the white women see how poorly her family lived compared to theirs. Mother Rose reassured her, baked a nice cobbler to take over, and loaned Emily her good china cups, her wedding gift from Catherine Jane and Wilbur. Catherine Jane was not part of the group—Wilbur wouldn't let her join, no surprise.

The day of the meeting Mother Rose and Emily made sure the house was spick-and-span. But then it rained, poured all day, and the unpaved streets turned to mud so slick and so sticky that it sucked the shoes right off your feet. When the white women arrived, they had to wade through all that mud to get into the house. Emily spread all the throw rugs she could find and then even her towels were on the floor, but it was still a mess.

"It gets like this every time it rains, I'm afraid," Emily apologized over and over to the white ladies, mopping and wiping up until she was ready to drop with exhaustion. She didn't have to explain a thing to the Negro women, who knew well enough what happened in The

Flats when it rained. In the spring, especially, the whole Negro part of town was partly submerged in gooey mud.

The white women lined up their ruined shoes by the door and padded around Emily's living room in their stocking feet. Mother Rose poured coffee into the fragile cups and handed them around. The ladies added cream—real cream, Mother Rose made sure of that—and served themselves sugar with Emily's silver-plated sugar spoon. Everything was done correctly, the way Rose Lee had learned at Mrs. Eunice Bell's.

"What y'all need out here," said Phoebe, stirring her coffee, "is to get your streets paved and some sidewalks put in. Best I know, this is the only part of Dillon that doesn't have paved streets."

That was how it started. Before the ladies left that evening, they had a plan. Phoebe would find out from her husband exactly what was needed to get the streets paved. She guessed the city had to approve it, and then the owners had to agree. They might have to cede to the city a narrow strip in front of each house. And there would be some cost, but it couldn't be that much, they thought. Each property owner would pay their share. The women decided they'd go in pairs, one black and one white, door to door, telling the neighbors about the plan.

Satisfied that they had a worthwhile project to work on, the women put on their muddy shoes and left. Mother Rose helped Emily clean up again. Washed and dried the thin white cups. Set aside the leftover cobbler for Julian and the children. Mopped up the muddy floor one more time.

Rains came and went. Mud turned to dust and back to mud again. The black-and-white pairs of women knocked on doors, explained and explained until they were worn-out, left pamphlets, went back again. Phoebe and Emily always went out together, and sometimes Mother Rose went with them, because she was so fond of Phoebe. Ned encouraged her.

"The Action Women" they were called in the neighborhood, sometimes not kindly. Not everybody liked having the white women coming around, "sticking their noses where they don't belong." Corny Overton was one who didn't like them, didn't like whites, *period*. But he was always cozying up to them, putting on an act that any fool should have been able to see right through; but he always seemed to pull the wool over the eyes of the white folk and many of the black, too.

Most people liked the idea of paved streets, but not everybody agreed. Some property owners couldn't be found. But Phoebe attacked the problem head-on. She went to the courthouse and looked up the names of the owners of every single piece of property in The Flats. Many, too many, were rent houses with landlords. Some landlords were black, like Cornelius Overton. Some were white, like Tom Plunkett, Phoebe's brother.

Phoebe found out that certain members of her rich white church, St. Mark's, owned property in The Flats, much of it neglected and trashy, including the several houses owned by her brother. She went around with a camera taking pictures of all those run-down properties and put them together in a big poster with a headline: THESE PROPERTIES ARE OWNED BY MEMBERS OF THIS CHURCH. She set up the poster in the entryway of St. Mark's. It caused a scandal, and for a long time Tom Plunkett refused to speak to his sister. On the other hand, the Negroes thought she was a heroine, almost unimaginably brave and foolish.

By and by most property owners agreed to pay their share and the city agreed to pay the rest, and streets in The Flats were mostly paved. One holdout was Cornelius Overton. He claimed it was because he didn't trust the city, telling people it was just a way for the city to take away some of their land that they'd worked and saved for. A lot of people believed him—it had happened before, hadn't it? *Remember Freedomtown!*

But Mother Rose knew Corny's real reason: He was cheap, that was all. So the strip of street in front of Overton's rent houses was the last to get paved. His tenants were still walking in the mud after the rest of the folks in The Flats were keeping their feet clean and dry. Then his wife's nephew began managing Overton's property and got it paved. About that time Cornelius started calling it Southeast instead of The Flats, as though improving the neighborhood had been his idea all along.

Mother Rose thought they'd come a long way from those days, but it seemed there was always *such* a long way to go. Gingerly she closed the door to that little room. She'd said enough about Tom Plunkett for now.

EIGHTEEN

The Wake

WHY DIDN'T MOM ever tell me about how scared she was when she went to the integrated school? And she'd never told me black kids weren't allowed to use the public library in Dillon. Could she have forgotten all that? Or had it always been too painful for her to remember?

Maybe part of the reason we had come to Dillon was for Mom to find what she had lost—the early pieces of it, before she moved away and the ties that connected her to who she was and where she came from were broken. But I didn't see how this was going to happen in only one more week. It would be nice, I thought, if we could stay longer.

Dad is always telling us stories about what it

was like when he was growing up. They are like family legends. There was the time he was fooling around and broke a plate from the precious set of dishes his grandmother had brought from France as a bride, and his mother cried practically nonstop for a week. Now we have those dishes, and when we use them on special occasions, Dad always tells the story of the missing plate.

Mom teases him about the dog he had when he was a kid, a black cocker spaniel named Sambo. "How racist can you get?" she says when he mentions the dog.

Dad agrees. "They weren't politically correct times," he says. "And it was my father who named him. Dad's a good guy, but not what you'd call a model of cultural sensitivity. Until we started educating him," he always adds with a smile.

One of his favorite tales is about his high school prom. He was too shy to get a date, so his friends fixed him up with a girl nobody liked. He bought her a corsage that made her sneeze and her eyes swell up, and then she stepped on the hem of her dress and ripped the whole thing apart. She made him take her home before the dance even started. I always laugh when he tells the story, even though I feel sorry for the poor girl.

But I don't even know if Mom went to a high school prom or if she had a dog or cat. It's like my dad's childhood has to do for both of them, because she misplaced hers along the way.

IT WAS TIME for the wake, and I was as ready as I was going to be. I don't know which I dreaded most—seeing a dead person or running into Brandy again. Cars had begun pulling into the parking lot. Mr. Phillips hovered near the door to make sure the older people made it up the steps safely. Mom steered me ahead of her, right behind Mother Rose, so I couldn't get away. There had been no problem convincing Robby to go—he was curious about everything involving the funeral business. He thought seeing Cornelius laid out in the Monarch was cool. That was a child's opinion, which I did not share.

People gathered in the hallway nodded respectfully and stepped aside for Mother Rose as she made her way into the slumber room. She joined a line that was filing slowly past the Overton family—including Brandy—who were clustered around the coffin and dabbing at their eyes with handkerchiefs. Everywhere you looked, there were flowers.

The line crept forward, and people murmured and pumped Marcus's hand and greeted the other relatives. I had never been to a funeral, and I was really scared to look in the casket. I decided that when I got close I'd shut my eyes or turn my head slightly and just *not look*. The sickly sweet smell of all those flowers was making me dizzy. I broke out in a cold sweat. I knew it was stupid to be scared of some dead old man in a coffin, but the closer I got to the body, the more spooked I became.

The line moved, and suddenly I found myself right next to Cornelius Overton, his eyes closed and his bony hands perched like crows on the ivory satin blanket that was pulled up to his chest. I stared at him. *Dead*, I thought. *Dead*.

Then I made the mistake of thinking about the room where Uncle James prepared the body, the metal table, the glass cabinet full of instruments, and the black rubber apron on a hook near the door. At that moment I thought I saw Corny's hand tremble, just a little, and his chest seemed to rise. I held my breath and stared harder, watching for another tremor, a sign that he wasn't dead after all. His eyelid fluttered—I'd swear it did. I stopped breathing.

And that's the last thing I remember.

I CAME TO on the sofa in the visiting parlor with Mom bending over me, holding something nasty-smelling under my nose. "You fainted,"

Mom said. "Breathe this and you'll be OK in a minute."

Robby gawked at me with huge eyes. "I thought you were *dead*," he said. "You dropped to the floor like a big rock."

I started to cry, I was so embarrassed. This was probably the most humiliating thing that had ever happened to me in my entire life, even worse than wetting my pants during my first—and last—violin recital in second grade. "Did I make a lot of noise?" I asked.

"Just a thump," Robby said. "You didn't moan or anything."

"Oh, Mom," I said, and then I *did* moan, "what must all those people think?" What I meant was, *What does Brandy think?* Answer: *That I'm even more of a dweeb than she originally believed, and she probably blames it on my white genes*.

"Emily Rose." It was Mother Rose. I turned my head away, too ashamed to look at her. "Don't you think a thing about it. That's why we always keep smelling salts handy. Lots of people just faint dead away, especially if they haven't been to funerals much. There's almost always somebody, isn't there, Todd?"

"That's right," said Mr. Phillips, lingering by the door. Another witness to my disgrace.

"Sweet child," Mother Rose continued, "it's nothing to be ashamed of. Mr. Overton's relatives have a lot more on their minds just now than thinking about you."

I could hear the taped organ music and the murmur of voices in the next room. Mr. Phillips said that an unusually large number of people had come to pay their respects, and he excused himself and returned to his post—in case somebody else keeled over and he had to whip out another vial of smelling salts.

I sat up. My head felt as though it was stuffed with dryer lint. "I'm going outside for a minute," I said, and Mom protested that it was too hot and I was probably still shaky. But I had to get away from the mournful music and the smell of flowers. I wanted fresh air, even if it was ninety-four degrees.

The hallway was crowded with mourners, the corners of their mouths pulled down. I half expected Brandy to step out of the slumber room and block my path. She didn't disappoint me.

"Emily Rose, what happened?" she asked. "I saw them carry you out. Did you get sick? What's the matter with you?"

"Nothing," I said, gritting my teeth. "I'm fine." I headed straight for the door and rushed outside.

Brandy followed right behind me. "I could walk around with you some, until you feel better," she offered.

I turned and faced her. "What is it with you, Brandy?" I demanded. "Yesterday you were full of nasty comments about my hair and my lips and how I talk. So I don't need you coming around today being nice just because you know I've got a good-looking brother." I stalked away from her and headed toward Morgan Street with no idea of where I was going. Mom was right; my legs were shaky. This might not have been such a good idea.

But Brandy caught up to me easily. "How 'bout if I apologize. I'm sorry. I shouldn't have said all that. But you do come on, you know, pretty snobbish. What you need is somebody to tell you what's what."

Brandy might have been ready to quit, but I wasn't ready to give up so easily. "Who asked *you*? And don't think you can apologize and then in the next breath tell me I'm snobbish."

She grinned at me. "You're turning out to be tougher than I thought. So—I'm sorry, *period*, and you're not snobbish. How's that?"

"OK," I said. We shook hands.

"So what happened?" Brandy asked again. She shortened her steps to match mine.

"I fainted, that's all. I've never been to a wake before," I confessed, gulping in damp air. "It sort of got to me, seeing the body."

"Never been to a wake before?" she asked incredulously. "Nobody in your family dies, or what?"

"Not since I've been old enough to remember."

That apparently amazed her, but she recovered. "So what do you do back in Connecticut? Like now, in the summer? You go to the beach and stuff?"

"Sometimes. But mostly my friend Alicia and I hang out at the nature center. Whenever people find injured animals, like birds and raccoons, they bring them to the nature center and we help take care of them. Our whole family goes there a lot. There's a skunk named Rosebud that's my special project. When I go back, I'm going to be a junior curator."

"So how long are you going to be here?" she asked. I noticed that her braids were arranged in a different way. Her plain black dress was short, and she wore a necklace of pretty glass beads.

"Another week," I said.

"Hey, you wanna go down to Green Acres? It's not such a great mall, to tell the truth. What

I wish we could do is go into Dallas to the Galleria. I bet you'd love it. My dad's new girlfriend takes me there sometimes."

"Your father has a girlfriend?"

"Yeah."

I didn't know what to say, so I said nothing.

"But Green Acres isn't too bad. We could catch a movie, get some pizza, look at clothes. Whatever."

I don't really like hanging out at the malls because I think they're pretty boring. But I didn't want to say that to Brandy and convince her that I was snobbish after all. In spite of her being so rude and arrogant, there was something about her. She'd kill me if she knew, but Brandy reminded me of Rosebud when I first found her in the woods, beautiful but injured and scared and trying so hard to spray to keep me away.

So I said I'd go. We made plans: Not the next day, which was the funeral, but the day after, Saturday, we'd take the old-fashioned trolleybus out to Green Acres.

Then we walked back to the funeral home. I was feeling better. Brandy didn't even *ask* about Steven, even though I knew she must be dying to. I had to give her points for that.

NINETEEN

Red Convertible

MOM DECIDED to wait up for Steven, and Robby and I were playing Monopoly to keep her company. Robby was winning big. Uncle James retired early to rest up for the funeral the next day, but Mother Rose, wrapped in a peach-colored bathrobe, was having another cup of tea, or maybe it was the same one she'd been sipping all evening.

"No need to wait up," Mom said. "I just want to make sure Steven gets in all right."

"I'm a regular night owl," Mother Rose said. "I always stay up past midnight. I might be in my room, but that doesn't mean I'm asleep."

Robby cut himself another slice of the angel food cake that had been brought over, along with a green Jell-O salad, by a couple of elderly ladies from Forgiveness Baptist who wanted to welcome us to Dillon. They'd hugged Mom and cried a little, because they'd known her when she was a little girl and they remembered her momma, who'd been their dear friend. "Don't stay away so long next time," they told her, "you and these precious children." There wasn't going to be much of the cake left when the precious children got through with it, but Mom made us save a piece for Steven.

Steven strolled in around eleven o'clock, surprised and not too pleased to find a welcoming committee. Naturally Robby couldn't wait to tell him about how I had fainted at the wake. "Just fell down, *crash*, like that."

"I did not *crash*. It was more like I crumpled."

"You OK now, Emmy?" Steven asked. I said I was.

"And how was your evening?" Mom inquired in an offhand way that didn't fool anybody. She was being careful not to *pry*, but she was curious. We all were, even Mother Rose.

"Oh, we had a great time. Marissa drove me around downtown, the courthouse square, and then out to the historic district."

"Did she show you the old Bell Mansion?" Mother Rose asked. "Big white house with an upstairs balcony and an iron fence all around it." She traced the outline in the air.

"Where the historical society has its museum, right? Marissa's mother does volunteer work there as a docent. But it was closed when we got there."

"I worked at that house, too, but it wasn't as any docent and I didn't volunteer," Mother Rose harrumphed. "That's where Catherine Jane Bell grew up."

"You worked there?" Steven asked. "In that mansion?"

"Indeed I did. I know every inch of that big old house, inside and out. But," she said, "don't let me interrupt."

"Wow," Steven said, "that's cool."

Cool! I thought. *Steven, you stupid jerk!*

He plunged on. "Well, then Marissa took me to her house. It's out in the country and just *huge*. The kitchen is bigger than this whole downstairs. All the rooms face a courtyard open on one side, and that's where the pool is."

"They must be awful rich," Robby said. He wasn't doing too bad, himself. All his wealth was in hotels on Park Place and Boardwalk.

"That's for sure. They've got a four-car garage. Marissa has her own BMW, which she's supposed to share with her brother, but he's up in Idaho for the summer. Mrs. Plunkett drives a Mercedes, and Dr. Plunkett has a Porsche *and* a Range Rover. Marissa's parents own part interest in a cutting-horse ranch somewhere north of here. She's taking me up there to see it."

"What's a cutting horse?" I asked Steven, who had discovered the angel food cake.

"Haven't got a clue. But I'll be able to tell you all about it Saturday," Steven promised, flashing us a big happy grin.

Mother Rose sighed and stood up. "Good night, children," she said, and headed off to her room.

"Yes," Mom said, "bedtime. Off you go, Rob. You, too, Emmy."

I was partway up the stairs when I heard Mom say, "Steven, sit down. We need to talk."

Robby kept going, but I crept back down to the bottom of the stairs to listen. Steven started to argue that he was tired, it had been a long day, and there was nothing to talk about.

Then Mom said in a voice I hardly ever hear her use, "*I said, sit down!*"

A chair scraped.

"Now listen to me," she said. "You are not in Northdale. You are not in the North, period. This is Texas. Marissa is white. You're black. And you're being extremely naive."

"Mom, we're not *doing* anything!"

"*You* know that. *She* knows that. But *they* don't know it."

"Who's 'they'?"

"Anybody who doesn't like the idea of a black boy and a white girl together. Her parents, for instance. And I'm warning you, there are lots and lots and *lots* of people who feel that way and may try to do something about it. Don't go asking for trouble."

"OK, Mom," Steven said, his voice coming closer. "Whatever you say. Good night."

I raced silently up the stairs and ducked into my room. *How come*, I wondered, *Mom didn't say, 'You're double,' like she always does at home? Did that all change when we came here?*

CORNELIUS OVERTON'S funeral was to take place at eleven o'clock Friday morning, and it could not be over with too soon to suit me. We'd arrived in Dillon on Tuesday and it was now Friday and it seemed most of the time and energy had been focused on getting Corny buried. It was like a ghost had come back to haunt Mother Rose, and she wouldn't be able to shuck it off until Corny was safely underground.

At breakfast Uncle James nervously munched plain toast and drank black coffee. There were, he explained, a thousand details involved in arranging a funeral. Mom had decided we didn't have to go, which was a huge relief. I was still feeling humiliated about fainting. Robby was on his way to visit his new friend Nathan and his tropical fish. Steven mentioned that Marissa was picking him up at the library. They were going to play tennis at her club and go swimming afterward.

Uncle James raised his eyebrows. "The library is a considerable walk from here," he commented. "Why not pick you up here?"

"It's easier that way," Steven insisted. "With the funeral going on today, she knows it's going to be busy around here. Next time maybe I'll ask her to stop here so I can introduce y'all."

"*Y'all?*" Mom echoed. "Introduce *y'all*? You've been here less than a week and you're already acquiring a Texas accent."

"How come you don't have a Texas accent, Mom?" Robby asked. "You were born here."

"I've still got a trace of it, if you listen carefully."

"But you don't say *y'all*."

"No," she said, "I don't. I don't say 'gonna' or 'huh?' either, please notice."

"But *how come*?" Robby insisted.

"In college I wanted to be on the debating team, so I signed up for a speech class. And I've never forgotten Professor Stein's lecture on the importance of enunciation, pronouncing words clearly. If your diction is sloppy, he used to tell us, people will either ignore you or underrate you. If you want to persuade people that what you have to say is valuable, you'd better speak correctly."

I thought about Brandy saying I have a prissy white way of talking, but I decided not to bring that up. Brandy was a complicated subject, and I wasn't exactly sure how Mother Rose would react to me going to the mall with Cornelius's great-granddaughter. I'd tell them about Brandy after things calmed down.

Later, I walked with Steven to the end of the driveway. He was going on and on about Marissa's red convertible—she'd let him drive it on the way back from the barbecue place. Steven had had his license for four months, since as soon after his sixteenth birthday as was legally possible, and he'd do almost anything for a chance to drive.

"Wait till you start to drive, Emmy," he said. "It is the greatest feeling in the world! What's even greater is getting behind the wheel of a superb driving machine like this beemer. And to have the top down and a beautiful girl beside you makes it just about perfect."

And it made me just about throw up. "More beautiful than Samantha?" I asked. I was being nasty, but I was also remembering the conversation I'd overheard the night before, and I was worried.

Steven looked away. "Different. They're two

different people. It's stupid even to compare them." He was mad that I'd brought it up, and I couldn't blame him—that's why I had done it. "Marissa is my *friend*, that's all. Samantha is my *girlfriend*. And, if you want to know the truth, Emily Rose"—he hardly ever uses my full name, and he didn't caress it the way Mother Rose did—"all of this is totally and completely none of your business."

End of conversation.

TWENTY

Sharing a Secret

I WATCHED from the window as Uncle James and Mr. Phillips wheeled the coffin out to the hearse. Uncle James was to drive it over to Forgiveness Baptist. Mr. Phillips would follow in the van, taking all of the flowers to the church, where everything had to be set up all over again. Ordinary funerals were usually held in the chapel, but since Uncle James expected a big turnout, Cornelius Overton's service would be held at Forgiveness.

Mother Rose, dressed all in black, a black straw hat set fiercely on her head, rode along with Uncle James. I thought that was interesting, considering the passenger in the back of the hearse.

With Robby gone to Nathan's and Steven off

at the country club, that left Mom and me by ourselves. Mom decided to test-bake a mocha cake for the cookbook she'd been thinking about writing. Whenever she had a few spare minutes, she'd get her spiral-bound notebook and start jotting down ideas. She called it *Café au Lait à la Carte*. All the recipes would have something to do with coffee: different kinds of coffee; things to eat with coffee, like dunking cookies; and things you could make with coffee, like this mocha cake, which used dark chocolate and espresso. Mocha cake is what I always ask for on my birthday.

"I hope Uncle James doesn't have to watch his cholesterol," Mom said, as six eggs plopped into the bowl. "I just put a quiche in the oven for lunch."

While Mom worked on the cake, scribbling notes as she went along, I sat at the table writing a letter to Alicia, to tell her what was going on here. Alicia is a double, too. Her father is from Nigeria and her mother is from England. They both have beautiful accents, but Alicia talks like me.

Mom scraped the batter into a pan and invited me to lick the bowl. "I need your advice on something, Em," she said, watching my finger work its way through the fudgy stuff. "As a fashion authority."

"Of course," I said, *lick*, *lick*, "I shall be glad to act as your wardrobe consultant."

"This is *serious*, girl," she said. "Uncle James has invited me to go with him to the W. E. B. Du Bois Reunion Banquet and Ball tomorrow night."

"But you didn't go to that school, Mom," I pointed out brilliantly.

"Well, that's true, but after all, my mother taught there. The banquet is part of the Diamond Jubilee, Uncle James is chairman, and he wants me to be his guest. Anyway, here's the problem: I have nothing to wear."

"What about the outfit you brought for Juneteenth? Can't you wear that?" She'd brought creamy silk pants and a top that she'd had for a long time but that still looked really elegant on her.

"This is a formal occasion. People in Dillon seem to get a lot more dressed up than people back home, have you noticed? I need a *gown*. Something that sparkles, maybe. Have any advice?"

"Could you borrow a dress from somebody?"

"I would, but I don't really *know* anybody. Back home I'd call Minda or Cheryl and the problem would be solved. But I don't have any girlfriends here."

"Maybe Brandy's mom would know."

"Brandy *who*, honey? I didn't even know you knew anybody."

"Brandy Woodrow. Mr. Overton's great-granddaughter. The really tall, *tall* girl who went for a walk with me after I fainted. Remember? We're going to the mall tomorrow."

Mom's eyebrows soared. "You are? To the mall? With Corny's great-granddaughter? I'll bet Mother Rose will have a word or two to say about that!" She laughed and shook her head.

"You don't think she'll be mad, do you? Mother Rose, I mean."

"Well, not at *you*. And maybe after today she can stop being so mad at him, too. Anyway, I'm glad you're going. But I can't just, you know, call up a total stranger and go, 'Hey, will you lend me a formal gown for Saturday night?' " Mom ran water into the mixing bowl, which hardly needed washing now that I was done with it. "Maybe you're right, Em. I'll just wear my silk outfit and hope it's OK."

Mom sat down at the table with me and began working on her recipe. The hard part, she told me, was not just getting the ingredients right—half a cup of this, a teaspoon of that—but explaining in a clear, simple way exactly how to put the ingredients together. Meanwhile, I continued with my letter, looking for a clear, simple way to explain to Alicia what it felt like being here, on the one hand being cherished by my family and on the other hand being looked at like a visitor from an alien planet—fitting perfectly and not fitting at all. I wondered how Alicia would react to Brandy and to being called a half-breed!

I wasn't even sure how *I* was reacting. But I found myself writing, "If I stayed here for the rest of the summer, maybe I'd get to feel like I *belong*." Then I stopped and thought, *Would I really want to do that—stay here after Mom left?*

I loved being here with Mom. She is always so busy at Café au Lait that we never have time just to hang out. For once I had her all to myself. Then I remembered Mother Rose's paintings. *It's your secret to share*, she'd told me.

"Mom?"

"Um-hmmmm?"

"When you've got a minute, I have something to show you."

She closed her notebook. "You've got me curious. Show me."

As I opened the door to Mother Rose's bedroom, I said, "It's all right. I have permission."

Mom gasped, just like I knew she would. And I explained what I remembered about the paintings and the stories they told about the people of Freedomtown and The Flats.

"This is incredible," she kept saying over and

over, "absolutely incredible." "The whole history of the African American part of Dillon is right here on these walls. Emily Rose, *these are our people*!"

"I know," I said, amazed all over again. *Our people!*

Then Mom discovered a painting that I hadn't really noticed before: a little black girl and an old woman walking toward a school building. White faces stare out of every window, and the little girl clutches the old woman's hand. "My God," Mom breathed. "Look at this."

"That's you." I reached for her hand and held it tight.

"Uh-huh." After a minute Mom took a deep breath. "Does anybody else know about these?" she asked.

"She didn't say."

"They ought to be in a museum somewhere. Something this precious shouldn't be kept a secret. They should be shared."

The kitchen timer rang. The mocha cake was done. I coaxed her for a tiny taste, but Mom had decided it would be her special contribution to the Sunday picnic.

Then Mother Rose and Uncle James came back from the funeral and ate some of the leftover green Jell-O salad with Mom's leek-and-spinach quiche. The topic of discussion was the funeral, which I gather had gone smoothly, but all the good things Pastor Hilton had to say about Cornelius Overton had Mother Rose in a snit. After lunch Uncle James changed clothes and left for Star Laundry and Dry Cleaners to fix a leaky washing machine, and Mother Rose went to her room to recuperate. I was sure Mom would say something about the paintings, but if she was waiting for the right moment, it didn't come. I kept thinking about what Mom had said, that the paintings should be shared. I wondered how Mother Rose would react to that idea.

While I was setting the table for supper, Steven breezed in, announced that he and Marissa were driving down to Lewisville, where he was going to help her shop for a new tennis racket, and rushed out again.

Mom opened her mouth, closed it, and bit her lip. I thought she'd give him another lecture about being careful because Marissa is white, but she didn't. Maybe she trusted him to use his head.

All afternoon the sky had been filling up with fat gray clouds that got darker and darker, and thunder rumbled ominously in the distance. Uncle James got home just before the massive storm broke. "Bad night to be on the road," he said, wiping his glasses. "We're in for a pounding."

Minutes later rain and hail rattled against the windows, lightning flashed and thunder boomed close by, and the wind blew over a huge tree in the front yard. Mom was a nervous wreck, wondering where Steven was, but just before all the lights went out, Steven called to say they were safe.

"He says they're at a mall," Mom reported, sounding relieved. "They're going to get something to eat and catch a movie until the storm's over. He said he might be late."

"Who's 'they'?" Uncle James asked. "Is he with the Plunkett girl?"

"Yes," Mom said, giving Uncle James a worried look.

"*Tch-tch,*" Uncle James clucked and shook his head. "Maybe I should have a talk with him."

"I've tried," Mom said. "He just doesn't realize."

"He will," Uncle James rumbled. "Sooner or later he will."

THE STORM had blown through and we'd finished supper when Dad telephoned, as he'd promised. Mom gave him a quick hello, and next Robby got on and told him all about

Nathan's tropical fish. Then it was my turn. I was anxious to hear my father's voice again.

"So what's new, Emily Rose?" he asked. He caressed my name almost the way Mother Rose did. "Lots," I said, but I didn't know where to begin. So I described the big storm and the tree in the front yard that Uncle James was now outside inspecting. "It was pretty exciting."

When I was finished, Dad asked to talk to Steven. I handed the phone back to Mom. Let *her* explain.

TWENTY-ONE

Green Acres

WHEN BRANDY arrived on Saturday morning, Mom had just announced that she'd stopped fretting about what to wear to the banquet that evening and had definitely settled on the cream-colored pants and top. "It's not formal, but it's good enough," she said. "It'll be appropriate."

I introduced Brandy to my mother, who was in the kitchen again, this time frying huge batches of chicken for the big picnic on Sunday. Mother Rose was there, too; she'd insisted on helping. Brandy was very polite, shaking Mom's hand and bobbing her head to Mother Rose. When I'd finally screwed up the courage to tell Mother Rose about Brandy, she told me she'd known Brandy since the day Brandy's parents brought her as an infant to Forgiveness Baptist. "I've watched 'em all grow up," Mother Rose said. "Some go this way, some that."

"Which way is Brandy going?" I asked curiously.

"The child has a good heart," Mother Rose said. "Her head will catch up."

Her mouth, too, I hope, I thought to myself.

I'd expected Brandy to show up dressed up like a fashion model, but she was wearing white bib overalls over a white T-shirt. She explained to me that this was exactly the kind of outfit Brandy—*the* Brandy—wears on the cover of her album. We were walking over to the trolley stop on East Avenue, stepping over the huge puddles left from the previous night's storm. "Your momma sure is pretty," Brandy said. "Nice hair. Is it all hers or does she get a weave?"

"Hers," I said. I didn't want to show ignorance by admitting I didn't know what a "weave" was. Brandy fascinated me, and I'd decided I wanted to get along with her, even though I could see that wasn't always going to be easy.

While we waited for the trolley, and then while we were riding to the mall, we talked about school and friends and the kinds of stuff we like to do. I told her about Alicia.

"Nigerian and British!" Brandy propped her

hands on her hips, elbows sticking out sharp as hooks. "What're people thinking about when they marry like that?" she marveled. "If there's one thing makes me furious, it's a black man going with a white woman, like we're not *good* enough for them."

"Maybe they just fall in love with each other," I snapped. "And they don't think about it at first, then after they do start thinking about it, it's too late." At least that was my theory, the way I thought it must have happened with my parents.

"No way I'd go out with any white boy," Brandy stated. "They're so, I don't know, *pale*. And that stringy-straight hair that just hangs there." She shuddered and made a face. "And those blue eyes are too weird, like there's nobody *in* there."

That really stung. I thought of my dad. He has straight brown hair and blue eyes, and he's not the least bit weird. In fact, I can't imagine a better person. "It's more complicated than that," I told her angrily. "It's more what's inside. I heard somewhere," I continued, "that skin color accounts for only about two percent of a person's genes. Hardly anything, when you think about it."

"Huh! Try telling that to some white guy that won't give you a job or tries to keep you from living in his neighborhood, like you even wanted to in the first place."

I hoped Mother Rose was right, that Brandy was good-hearted, because she sure did have a wicked tongue. It was a relief to get to Green Acres Mall and away from an uncomfortable subject, although that didn't mean I stopped thinking about what she'd said. If I went along with Brandy's view, I'd have to start thinking of myself as black and the white part wouldn't count. That would be like rejecting my dad and saying *he* didn't count.

This was going around and around in my head when we stopped in a music store so Brandy could check out the new releases.

"You like rap?" Brandy asked.

"I like R & B better."

She gave me a look that I was sure said, "That means you don't like rap and you're too chicken to say so, but I'm going to let it pass." She was right.

We searched for the kind of white cap that *the* Brandy wears on her album. We ate corny dogs from a booth in the food court, and I gave away my Yankee-ness again by being totally ignorant of this deep-fried hot dog coated with cornmeal.

Everything about me seemed strange to Brandy. She thought Silver Hill Country Day

School sounded bogus. When I tried to tell her about their terrific scholarship program and how they go out of their way to recruit minority kids and have a faculty that reflects the racial makeup of our area, she laughed. She teased me about the way I talk but didn't seem to notice that I had to keep asking her to repeat because I couldn't make out what she was saying half the time.

"You're the one with the accent," I said, "not me."

"*Me?* You gotta be kiddin' me. No way I got any accent."

"Sure you do. Even my brother Steven is picking up a Texas accent. Mom heard him say 'y'all' the other day and had a fit."

"You serious? Threw a fit 'cause he said 'y'all'?"

"Not really. Just a minor lecture."

She asked me what kind of sports I played. I told her I belong to an ice-skating club and during the school year I practice twice a week at an indoor rink. "I *knew* we should have figured out a way to get into Dallas! Right in the middle of the Galleria they've got a rink where you can ice-skate even when it's a hundred degrees outside. You could teach me how to do those jumps and spins and stuff."

We kept trying to find something we felt the

same way about. It was like we talked different languages about practically everything. When she asked about church and I told her about St. Brigid's, she just shook her head. Then she asked what I wanted to do when I grew up. I told her I wanted to be a photographer for the Discovery Channel and to go to Africa to study wild animals.

"That's what you think Africa is for?" she demanded, eyes narrowed. "That's where your ancestors come from, girl, same as mine. On slave boats. In chains! I guess you just want to think that Africa is where lions and tigers come from, and *your* ancestors come from France!" She had already gone too far, and then she went one long step further. "You know," she said thoughtfully, "it must feel really creepy to have a white daddy."

I chose to ignore her remark about our ancestors in Africa, but this last remark made me mad. It seemed all we were going to do was fight, and I didn't hesitate. "You know what's even creepier than having a white father?" I asked softly. "It's having a father who lives with a girlfriend in Dallas."

She looked as though I'd slapped her. *Good*, I thought.

The next minute I felt bad for her. "I'm sorry," I said.

She sniffled and wiped her nose. "I miss him," she said. "I miss us being together."

"I know," I said. I was missing my dad, and we'd only been gone for a week. "I'm sorry," I repeated. "How about a truce? You don't mock my family, and I don't mock yours."

"OK," she said.

So then, to change the subject, I asked Brandy what she wanted to do when *she* grew up.

She turned a smile on me like a three-hundred-watt halogen bulb. "Sing," she said. "I'm going to be a famous singer someday."

I got the picture. "Like Brandy Norwood."

"Right. I'm taking singing lessons. I sing with the Uptown Girls at our high school. I'm the youngest one. Usually they don't let anybody join in the middle of the year, but our choir director at church told them I was real good, and they let me in. Soon as I'm sixteen I'm going to audition for the North Texas Gospel Choir. They have a scholarship program that might help me with college, if I want to go. I can do gospel, R & B, rap, whatever." She heaved a sigh. "My momma wants me to go to library school," Brandy said, "in case the singing career doesn't work out. She's a school librarian."

"That would be cool," I said. "When you

think that your momma probably wasn't even allowed to use the Dillon library when she was growing up."

She looked at me sharply—surprised, I guess, that I knew such a thing. "Momma says if not a librarian, then a teacher. But not me, no way. My little sister, LaTrisha, is such a pain! I'm probably never going to have any kids myself, unless I'm rich enough to hire a nanny to take care of them."

We checked out makeup at JCPenney and tried on shoes at the Bootery. We stopped in at Lone Star Souvenirs and I bought a coffee mug for my dad—dark blue with white letters that read LONDON ROME PARIS DILLON—and a notepad in the shape of a cowboy boot for Alicia. I also found a postcard showing the courthouse on the square to send to Rosebud, c/o Northdale Nature Center.

"You sending a postcard to a *skunk*?" Brandy hooted.

"It's just a *joke*, Brandy."

"Huh. You are some weird Yankee girl, I'll say that."

"And you are some weird Texan," I shot back. The trick with Brandy, I discovered, was not to let her get away with a thing. It also helped to remember how long it took to tame Rosebud.

We tried on sunglasses at a cart, talked to the

parrot on a perch outside the pet store, and bought frozen yogurt cones with sprinkles and sat on a park bench to eat them. Brandy kept looking for someone she knew. Some girls sauntered by and waved, but none stopped to talk. I had already spent the five dollars Mom gave me plus some of my own.

"Might as well go home, then," Brandy sighed. "None of my friends hangin' here today anyhow."

We were walking toward the exit when I saw an evening gown in the window of an expensive shop. The top was black and tight-fitting above a floaty white skirt.

"You seeing yourself in that dress, Emily Rose?" Brandy asked. "Think you got enough chest to hold it up?"

"I'm seeing my *mom* in it," I said. "She's going to the W. E. B. Du Bois Banquet tonight with Uncle James, and she doesn't have a dress. She says she's going to wear the outfit she brought for Juneteenth, but I think she'd really like something like this."

"My auntie Lu'Rae could fix her up like *that*," Brandy said, snapping her fingers. "Auntie Lu'Rae sews African dresses and shirts, and she does braids, too. She runs a shop there in her house. She's got customers driving up from

Dallas and Fort Worth. I bet she's got something your momma would love."

"Even if she does, though, Mom doesn't really have any money to spend on a dress she'd only wear one time."

"What makes you think she'd only wear it one time?" Brandy asked. " 'Cause nobody in Connecticut does African?"

"She doesn't go out that much," I said, irritated because I had to keep defending everything I said. "She works nights in her restaurant, every night but Sunday. And even if she did, my parents don't go out to formal things."

But Brandy insisted we get off the trolleybus one stop early to visit Auntie Lu'Rae. "It won't hurt just to look, will it?" she demanded when I tried to talk her out of it. The front porch of a brick house had been enclosed and an oval sign hung in one of the windows, looping letters that said LU'RAE DESIGNS. Brandy sailed right in. I followed reluctantly.

It might have been an ordinary hot, muggy day in Texas, but inside Lu'Rae Designs it was a hot, muggy day in Africa. Grass mats and carved ebony masks covered the walls. A ceiling fan turned slowly. Bright-colored cushions were strewn around on the floor, and a low table was piled with fashion magazines featuring black models. In one corner a dress dummy wore a gorgeous red satin robe with glittery designs embroidered down the front and around the sleeves.

"Sugarbabe, come right on in here!" A very big, dark woman with a head full of braids stepped out from behind a screen at one end of the room. "I'm doing Rhonda's braids for her, for the big banquet tonight. Who's this you brought with you, hon?"

Brandy introduced me. "This here is Emily Rose, down from Connecticut for the Jubilee. She's Mother Rose's girl."

Auntie Lu'Rae threw back her big head and beamed at me, a huge smile with two rows of square white teeth. "Thought I'd seen you someplace! Must have been at church the other night, that right? Well, we are so glad to have you here, and that beautiful momma of yours and your two fine-looking brothers. You having yourself a good time? My little niece showing you the sights? Come on back here and meet Rhonda. She's probably a relation of yours."

There was a chair and a stool behind the screen. In the chair sat a woman with a towel around her shoulders. Half the woman's head was in braids. The rest of her short, bunchy hair poked out in all directions. It turned out that this Rhonda, a thin woman with light brown skin and freckles on her long, narrow face, really was related to me. Her grandmother was Mother Rose's younger sister, Nancy Lee.

Auntie Lu'Rae perched her big behind on the narrow stool and went back to work on Rhonda. This was old stuff to Brandy, but I'd never seen anybody making braids before, and I edged up for a closer look. While Rhonda and Auntie Lu'Rae asked me questions about where I lived and all that, Auntie Lu'Rae's fingers never slowed down. She'd section off a little bit of Rhonda's short hair, snatch up a piece of fake hair from a pile on a table, twist it together with Rhonda's own hair, braid it, and then singe the end with her cigarette lighter. Her long fingernails were painted a deep purple.

Rhonda checked her watch. "I got to be home by five."

"You'll make it, and to spare," Auntie Lu'Rae assured her.

It wasn't quite two o'clock yet. "What time did you start?" I asked.

"Nine this morning I was in this chair," Rhonda said.

"Takes around eight hours. If Rhonda didn't drink about three gallons of iced tea and then have to run to the bathroom every half hour, we'd get done faster," Auntie Lu'Rae said.

"You gonna tell her what your momma

needs?" Brandy asked me. I opened my mouth and shut it again, trying to think what I was going to say, but Brandy couldn't wait. "Her momma needs an outfit for the banquet," Brandy told Auntie Lu'Rae. "I said you'd help her out."

"Got nothing to wear, that it?" Auntie Lu'Rae grinned her big-toothed grin at me.

"Nothing *formal*," I explained. "She has a nice outfit she brought for Juneteenth; it's really pretty, but it's not—"

"She needs something to show the local folks that black folks from Connecticut know how to dress up," Brandy cut in.

"Well, sugar, listen, why don't you just take her that red robe out there on the dummy and tell her to put it on over her pretty little outfit. Nobody gonna be wearing nothing like *that*, I can tell you. And if your momma don't wear it, it's just gonna stand there all by its lonesome like Cinderella while everybody else is at the prince's ball."

I was stunned. This red robe looked like something from a museum, something an empress would wear. "I don't think my mother would... I mean, she wouldn't want to borrow something that, uh, that expensive... because, what if something happened, like she spilled something on it?"

"Then she just takes it over to Star Laundry and Dry Cleaning and lets James worry about it! No problem there, sugar."

Brandy was already undressing the dummy and folding up the red robe. "You got a bag I can put this in, Auntie Lu'Rae?"

"Get a sheet out of the closet there, Brandy. Just be sure to hang it up when you get it over to Mother Rose's, understand? Too bad I don't have time to do your momma some braids for tonight. That outfit just calls out for braids."

"Let's go," Brandy said. "I can't wait to see your momma's face when she gets a look at this."

She had me out of there before I even had time to thank Auntie Lu'Rae the way she ought to be thanked. Brandy insisted on carrying the red robe as we walked all the way to the funeral home without a speck of shade to save us from the blazing Texas sun.

TWENTY-TWO

The Banquet

I COULDN'T IMAGINE going up to somebody's mother—even somebody I knew, let alone a total stranger—and telling her what to wear. But that's what Brandy did.

Mom was sitting at the kitchen table, working on her cookbook. Mother Rose was in her room—she made up for staying up late by taking a nap in the middle of the afternoon. Robby and Nathan and a couple of Nathan's cousins who had just driven up from Port Arthur for the weekend had gone swimming at Center Park pool. I don't know where Uncle James was. The house smelled of fried chicken.

" 'Scuse me, Miz Chartier," Brandy said, and she laid the long bundle out on the table in front of Mom and began undoing the sheet.

I could hardly wait to see how Mom was going to react when she saw it. "My auntie Lu'Rae sent this over for you to wear to the banquet tonight." She whipped off the sheet and stood back proudly. The red satin robe gleamed on the table.

"Good Lord," Mom breathed. "What *is* this? It's incredible."

"Auntie Lu'Rae makes 'em. African robes for special occasions. This is the one she keeps on display in her shop. And she's lending it to you for tonight, since you don't have something special to wear."

I could see that Mom didn't get it. She stammered and stuttered and protested, and Brandy just brushed her off. "Stand up," she commanded. "Let's see how this goes on you."

Mom was wearing her usual khaki shorts and cotton shirt. Her long hair was fastened at the back of her neck with a barrette. No jewelry, except her gold wedding band, and no makeup. No shoes, either—her leather sandals were under the table. Slowly she stood up, as though she were hypnotized, under Brandy's spell, and allowed Brandy to put the robe on her. The cut of the robe was very plain—long, wide sleeves, a stand-up Chinese-style collar, and covered buttons that fastened with little loops from the collar all the way down to the knees. The red satin was lined with black silk, and it was embroidered with black and gold ribbons in a pattern that Brandy said Auntie Lu'Rae told her was based on African tribal designs.

Brandy buttoned the little silk-covered buttons. From somewhere she pulled out a red headband that matched the robe and tied it around my mother's hair, letting the ends dangle over her shoulder. "There," Brandy said, stepping back. "Got a mirror?"

There was one by the door, where Uncle James always checked his appearance before going to his place of business. Mom let herself be led over to it. She raised her arms and turned around slowly, watching herself in the mirror. She looked so beautiful! I wished Dad could see her. All I could say was, "Wow, Mom!"

Then she came out of her spell. "Well, Brandy, it's fabulous, an incredible work of art, and I want you to thank your aunt for me, but of course I wouldn't dream of borrowing anything this valuable. I wish I could just *buy* it from her..." And she went on like that, protesting.

"She won't like it, Auntie Lu'Rae won't, if you don't wear her robe," Brandy said. "She's likely to take it as an offense that you say no."

Mom was still standing there in the beautiful robe, not really wanting to take it off, when

Mother Rose came out of her room. Mother Rose looked it over and turned to Brandy. "That Lu'Rae's work?" she asked.

"Yes, ma'am," Brandy said respectfully, bobbing her head.

"Fit for a queen," Mother Rose said. "You must wear it, Susan." And that settled it.

I went outside with Brandy, thinking she was about to leave. But she hung around and hung around, until she finally broke down and asked, "Where's your brother Steven?" as though she was asking about Robby or some other child.

"Out somewhere," I told her vaguely. No way I'd tell her he was out with a white girl! "He probably won't get back until *very* late."

She looked disappointed, and soon after that she left, saying she had to go home and babysit her little sister while her mother went to the banquet with Uncle Marcus and Aunt Aurelia. There had been an argument about going. Marcus didn't think it was the proper thing to go out to a big party so soon after the death of Cornelius Overton, but her mother and Aurelia argued that Cornelius had wanted to live to see the big Jubilee celebration and he would have wanted them to go. They compromised—they'd go for the dinner but wouldn't stay for the dancing afterward.

"See you in church tomorrow," Brandy said.

Off she went on her long, long legs, and I went back inside to take another look at the gorgeous robe.

MOM AND UNCLE JAMES were to leave for the Dillon Inn at six o'clock. Although Mother Rose had been invited to attend the W. E. B. Du Bois Banquet as an honored guest, she had refused.

"I'm a night owl, but I'm not much for parties," she said. "They're too noisy for me. Besides, I would much rather stay home with my Emily Rose."

MY Emily Rose. I loved that.

Mother Rose and I watched Mom go out wearing the flame red robe over her plain silk pants. Even if Mom hadn't gone to a prom when she was in high school, I thought, she was making up for it now. Uncle James looked very dignified in a white tuxedo. That was kind of a shock, after seeing him in nothing but black for the past few days. Robby was staying overnight with Nathan and his cousins, so Mother Rose and I settled down contentedly to supper by ourselves: two pieces of the fried chicken intended for the picnic and the last of the Jell-O salad.

We were in her room looking at her paintings again—me asking more questions, her telling more stories—when the phone rang. "You want to get that for me, Emily Rose? Can't imagine who it might be. I hope it's not a call for James, to spoil his evening."

It wasn't for James. It was a collect call from Steven Chartier. The operator pronounced it funny. I accepted the call, and Steven came on. "Emmy? Is Mom there?"

He sounded far away and kind of strange. I got a bad feeling as soon as I heard his voice. "No, she and Uncle James are at the banquet." Ignoring the bad feeling, I rushed on. "Steven, it's too bad you weren't here to see her! Brandy's auntie Lu'Rae loaned her this absolutely gor—"

Steven cut me off. "Emily, listen to me. I'm at the juvenile detention center at the courthouse in Slagerville. You've got to find Mom and have her come up here and get me."

Juvenile detention center? "Steven, are you serious? Where *are* you?"

"It's at the county jail in Slagerville. About twenty miles north of Dillon. It's all a bad mistake, but they won't listen to me. Here's the address—write it down, Em, please?"

I wrote down what he told me. "Steven, what happened?"

"I can't tell you now. Can you get ahold of Mom right away?"

"I will," I promised.

"Good girl, Emmy," he said. "I got to go now." He hung up.

I was shaking, and I started to cry. Mother Rose came out of her room. "Emily Rose, is that—" and then she saw my face. "What's wrong?"

"It's Steven," I sobbed. "He's in jail someplace, and I don't know why."

"Jail! Sit down, child," she said. "Tell me about it." She made me sit at the table, and she took my hand and asked me careful questions until she knew as much as I did. "Wonder where Marissa Plunkett is," she mused. "Did he say?"

"He didn't mention her," I said tearfully.

"We need to get in touch with your momma," Mother Rose said. "Do you think you can call her at the banquet?"

We looked up the number of the Dillon Inn, and I telephoned and asked the woman who answered the phone to get a message to Susan Chartier, telling her to call home immediately, *urgent*. We waited. Ten minutes crept by, while I tried not to go completely to pieces, and I called again. This time I said I'd hold on while someone went to find her, but then I got cut off. "Maybe I should have asked them to get Uncle James," I wailed. I was getting pretty frantic.

Mother Rose decided it was time for action.

"I'm going to call a taxi," she announced, "and we will go there ourselves and find them." She looked at me closely. "Wash your face," she said. "And comb your hair."

Minutes later Overton Taxi arrived, pulling up at the side entrance. Mother Rose already had her handbag and had pinned on her black straw hat. We climbed into the backseat. The driver smiled. "Hello, Mother Rose. Where you two ladies off to?"

"Hello, Byron. The Dillon Inn," she said. "My great-granddaughter and I are going to drop in on the banquet."

"Air conditioning's died on me," Byron apologized. "But we'll be there in a couple minutes." The noisy old taxi rattled across town, windows down, hot sticky air pouring in. It seemed to take forever to get there.

You're being extremely naive. Don't go asking for trouble.

He just doesn't realize.

He will, sooner or later.

At last the taxi delivered us to the main entrance. We made our way through the crowded lobby of the hotel to the ballroom at the end of the hall. We kept being stopped by people who knew Mother Rose and wanted to say hello. I could hardly talk, but somehow Mother Rose stayed calm and spoke politely to each one.

Music was playing, and people were laughing and talking. Everybody was dressed up, some of the men in tuxedos, some in African-style robes, and the women looked like exotic birds in their brightly colored dresses. Finally we spied Mom in her flame red robe.

"What's wrong? What's happened?" she said when she saw me.

"Now take it slow and tell her," Mother Rose said softly.

With the party swirling all around us, I managed to tell Mom what I knew in a voice choking with tears. Mom covered her face with her hands. "Let's find Uncle James. Do you see him anywhere? I've got to go up there right away."

We found Uncle James at the head table, getting ready to start the program as master of ceremonies. Mom made me repeat my story, which I managed to do a little more calmly. Uncle James nodded gravely. "I was afraid of something like this," he said.

"If I could just borrow your car, Uncle James," Mom begged. "No need for you to leave the banquet. If we're not back by the time it's over, maybe somebody could drive you home."

But Uncle James was not buying that. "Susan, you don't for a moment think I'd let you go up there alone, do you? I know very well how these small-town sheriffs operate. If you'll give me a few minutes to find someone else to take over as master of ceremonies, we'll drop Mother Rose and Emily Rose off at home, and then I'll drive you up to Slagerville myself."

"Not on your life," Mother Rose said firmly. "This is a family matter. We're all going." She looked at me. "You, too, Emily Rose."

I could have hugged her.

"All right," Mom said, too worried and upset to argue. "Let's go."

TWENTY-THREE

Prayer

LORD JESUS, Mother Rose prayed, her fingers making a little cage in her lap and her eyes shut tight against the world, *Lord Jesus, I am asking you to take care of these children, these innocent lambs who come here with open and trusting hearts.*

Mother Rose had not lost her faith in prayer. For years now she had carried on a running conversation with God's Only Begotten Son. It was easier to talk to Jesus than to go directly to Almighty God and tremble before His throne, that was her feeling. *Take it to the Lord in prayer*, Momma used to tell her, and Grandmother Lila before that. The men liked to preach—she thought of Ned's passionate sermons—and the women liked to sing, but praying was everybody's business.

Mother Rose sat in the backseat of James's Lincoln, which was heading straight as an arrow for the Slager County jail. The child beside her, her own Emily Rose, was chewing on her fingernail. A bad habit; it meant she was upset, nervous. *We are all upset*, Mother Rose thought. *Lord, have mercy*.

James and Susan had not even bothered to stop at home to change out of their finery. Susan looked like royalty in that red silk robe. But wouldn't Lu'Rae Brown have a fit if she knew her robe was on its way to the jail! Mother Rose smiled at the idea, knowing Lu'Rae, but she was careful to turn her head so Emily Rose wouldn't notice she was tickled about something.

She thought of her brother Henry. How many times she thought of Henry! Poor Henry, dead now for sixty years, and what a waste of intelligent manhood that had been! She remembered the last time she saw him, hidden beneath a counterpane in the backseat of Catherine Jane's poppa's automobile and mad as a hornet that his escape to Blue Springs had been arranged by women, including his sister and his aunt and a young white girl.

I wanted to go with them, Mother Rose remembered, *and they wouldn't let me*.

Now here she was, rushing along the big superhighway that ran to the west of the narrow, twisty old road through Blue Springs. They wouldn't pass through Blue Springs, but she'd soon be able to spy it off in the distance, beyond a little rise dotted with dark green trees.

Nobody was talking much. Every now and again James would murmur something to soothe Susan. From where she sat, Mother Rose could not see past James's broad shoulders to read the speedometer, but she knew he would not exceed the speed limit. No sense getting a ticket. Steady in all things, that was James. Just like his father, the professor. Certainly not like his momma—all fire and ice was Susannah Jones!

Her mind strayed back to Henry. Whenever Mother Rose thought of Henry, she thought of the trouble he got into, every time he turned around, it seemed. A hothead, that's what Henry was—didn't have the sense to stay out of the path of white folk and their ways.

Mother Rose wondered if perhaps Steven was like that. She didn't get that feeling, though—more that he was just a good boy, but maybe not tough enough, not "street-smart," as they say nowadays. It seemed none of these children had the least idea what it meant to be black. And they were *black*, even with all of Susan's talk about "biracial this" and "double that." What nonsense! All you had to do was look at them, three beautiful children, and you knew you were seeing three beautiful *black* children.

When Rose Lee Jefferson was a very young girl she already knew that a single drop of Negro blood meant you were Negro. Black folk knew it; white folk knew it. She'd been acquainted with two or three who tried to pass, thought life would be easier being white, but they found it wasn't so easy after all. Keeping the secret of that single drop was the hard part. Her friend Bessie's brother Lionel was so light-skinned and thin-lipped and straight-haired he got away with it for years. But it got too much for him. Lionel divorced his white wife and married a woman black as midnight.

It was none of her business how Susan brought up her youngsters, of course. *Maybe*, Mother Rose thought, *it's different up there in the North. Maybe Connecticut has a different attitude toward black folk. I hope so, for their sake*. Mother Rose had never been north, not in her whole life. She'd been to Oklahoma and Louisiana and most everywhere in Texas, except over there by El Paso where so many people talked Spanish, even up into Arkansas once. But when she was young and wanted to travel it was so hard, you couldn't even stop to use the toilet, just had to jump behind some bushes, if you could find any.

And be sure to pack your own food and your own water, too, or you'd be out of luck.

She heard it was different now. Black folk could go anywhere in the whole country and visit the rest room or order up a meal in a fancy restaurant if you felt like it and nobody would say one word to you. But she was too old now for that sort of travel. She used to like to visit some of Ned's cousins over in Shreveport, but not even that seemed such a good idea anymore. Home was best.

So what kind of trouble had young Steven got himself into? She had a pretty good idea it had something to do with the white girl, the Plunkett child—what was her name? Marissa Plunkett. Probably made somebody mad. That much hadn't changed. If her father knew she was keeping company with a Negro boy, he'd probably throw a fit, lock her in her room for the duration. *No different from his poppa, Tom Plunkett, in that regard*, she thought. *Bad news, both of them. And probably the girl, too.*

James slowed as they approached the outskirts of Slagerville. The fat cupola on top of the Slager County courthouse loomed ahead. They had Steven in there. Heaven only knew why. *Help us, blessed Jesus. Help us!*

TWENTY-FOUR

High Valley Ranch

I WANTED TO GO inside the ugly brown building with Mom and Uncle James and find out what had happened to Steven, but they made me wait in the car with Mother Rose.

"We'd just be in the way," Mother Rose said. "Anyway," she added, "I don't want to be around those people any more than I have to."

I don't know how long we waited. It seemed like hours. It was hot in the car without the air conditioning, and I was thirsty. "Let's go inside and get a drink of water," I suggested. "Maybe they'll let us sit in there where it's cool."

"Last time I was inside that courthouse," Mother Rose said, "they had two drinking fountains. One was nice and clean and had a sign that said whites only above it. The other was the dirty old leaky faucet outside the back door that had a colored only sign above it. Now that, I grant you," she continued, "was a long time ago. I still remember that. Sure do."

I decided I could do without.

Eventually, when the light was fading but the heat was as fierce as ever, the door opened and they came out: Uncle James in his white tuxedo, Mom in her flame red robe, and my brother Steven. I jumped out of the car when I saw them.

Steven looked terrible. The new jeans he'd put on that morning were dirty and torn. His cheek was bruised and one eye was swollen shut. His white shirt was spattered with blood from a bloody nose and a split lip.

Mom's mouth was pinched into a tight line.

"What happened?" I managed to ask.

"Got in some trouble," Steven mumbled, and gingerly touched his lip. He crawled into the back of the car.

"Did somebody beat you up?"

"Yeah."

"Enough questions, Emmy," Mom pleaded. "Why don't you sit up front with Uncle James, Mother Rose," she said, "and I'll sit back here with Steven."

I scrunched into one corner, making up my mind I wouldn't say another word if it killed me.

Mom perched in the middle. Steven slumped into the opposite corner and closed his other eye.

"What do you think, Steven?" Uncle James asked, peering in the rearview mirror. "Should we go straight to the hospital and have you examined?"

Steven shook his head. "I'll be OK," he said. "Just tired. And hungry. I haven't had anything to eat since breakfast."

"Then I propose that we go straight home," Uncle James said. "Susan? Agreed?"

"Yes," Mom said. "Fine." Then she added, "I should have brought along something for you to eat. Why didn't I think of that?"

Steven patted her arm. "Because you can't think of absolutely everything, Mom. Relax."

Relax! I thought. *You've scared everybody half to death and now you're telling us to relax!*

Uncle James drove back to Dillon as cautiously as he had driven up. Steven slept, I guess. Nobody talked. A million questions churned in my head.

After we got home, Mom and Uncle James checked Steven's eye, his cut lip, and his other bruises and decided some antiseptic would take care of it. While Steven went upstairs to take a shower, Mom laid the flame red robe on Mother Rose's bed and began fixing Steven an omelette.

Uncle James hung his tuxedo jacket over the back of his chair and turned up the cuffs of his starched shirt. Mother Rose changed into house slippers. We all sat down at the table and waited.

"Now," Mom said the minute Steven appeared. "Tell us exactly what happened."

"Start at the beginning," Uncle James said sternly, and I noticed that he had a lined yellow pad on the table in front of him. "Don't leave anything out."

Mom set a plate in front of Steven, and he dug in. "Well, to begin with," he said, between mouthfuls, "it was Marissa's idea for me to drive her beemer. She knew I was aching to get my hands on the wheel, even though I hadn't said a word. When she offered I even asked her, 'You sure it's OK? Your parents won't mind?' And she said something like, 'It's my car.' Then she suggested we take the back road up through Blue Springs, instead of the interstate. That was fine with me. Top down, nice cool breeze, and man, can that beemer corner! I loved it!"

Steven went on and on about that stupid convertible. I thought it was sickening. "So is that why you got arrested?" I interrupted. "For speeding?"

"No," Steven said, "it wasn't."

"Hush, Emmy," Mom said. "Let him tell his story."

"It's really pretty up there." Steven continued. "Not as many trees as we've got in Connecticut, but lots of rolling green hills. You know you're getting close to High Valley Ranch when you see miles of white pipe fence. Then you come to a huge iron gate with silhouettes of horses. After you punch in a code, the gate opens electronically, and you go up a road that winds past rows of tall, narrow trees. The ranch house is hidden in a grove of trees, but you can see the stables and other buildings and the outdoor ring as you drive up.

"On the way up Marissa told me all about the ranch, which is kind of a hobby for rich doctors. There's a neurosurgeon from Dallas—he and Dr. Plunkett were roommates at medical school—and another doctor from Houston who flies his own plane up and lands on the private airstrip. The three of them bought this ranch together as a place to go and relax on weekends, and the rest of the time a manager lives on the ranch. His name's Jasper."

Steven dabbed at his mouth with a napkin and took a long drink of juice. I tried to be patient, but Steven does love to dramatize.

"Marissa's been going to High Valley with her

folks for years, and she's known Jasper, and his wife, Rita, practically forever. And this is what I still don't get at all: 'Jasper's really a great guy,' Marissa told me. Her exact words. Maybe to her he is. He taught her how to ride and everything—how to groom a horse and take care of the tack. She made him sound like part of the family."

"Jasper," Uncle James interrupted. "Is that his Christian name or his surname?"

Steven looked confused. "Uh, I don't know. She just called him Jasper." Uncle James printed JASPER in capital letters on his yellow pad and underlined it twice.

"Anyway, we parked the car at Jasper's house and let him know we were there. He's a tall, lanky, leathery-looking guy, not much on smiling. *Gruff*, you know? I didn't think much about it at the time—he just seemed like kind of a character. Then Marissa took me around to show me the vet barn, one whole building just for veterinary stuff. And next we went to the stables to see the horses. They're cutting horses, specially bred for cowboys to ride when they separate out the calves from the rest of the herd. A cutting horse is very smart, she said, very quick and agile. I don't know anything about horses, but these looked like really beautiful animals."

Steven had finished his omelette. Silently Mom took away his plate and brought him another glass of juice.

"So then we went up to the show barn. There's this gallery on the second floor with a bar and a huge glass window overlooking the barn floor, which is covered with sawdust. There are heads of all kinds of animals staring at you from behind the bar, and the bar stools are actually real leather saddles. There's a big chandelier made entirely of antlers, and the chairs are covered in hide with the hair still on it. The whole thing was gross in a way, but unreal, kind of like a movie set."

I was getting irritated with Steven's long story. Now he was describing the interior decoration! "Who *cares* about the stupid antlers," I grumbled. "I want to know what happened."

Mother Rose smiled knowingly at me. "I suspect we'll find out in good time," she said. "Your brother has suffered, and if he needs to tell his story this way, then we need to listen."

Steven nodded to Mother Rose. "Thank you. I'm telling you all this because I think you need to understand the exact circumstances. Otherwise, Emily Rose, you'll be asking me questions all night and we'll never get to bed." I slumped down in my chair and chewed on my thumbnail.

"We went up to the gallery and goofed

around. There was nobody else in the barn, as far as we knew. I was sitting on a bar stool and giving my best John Wayne impression, saving the town from cattle rustlers. 'Waaal, Miz Plunkett,' I drawled, 'if thur's ennythin' Ah kin do to hep you—'

"Marissa wasn't sure if she wanted to be a schoolteacher or a saloonkeeper, so she was playing a little of both. She came out from behind the bar and stood beside me. 'Kiss me, cowboy,' she said, batting her eyelashes like mad. I just looked at her, not sure if we were still acting or what. Now you got to believe this: Up to then I hadn't touched her, not even to hold her hand. I'd thought about it, but up to then it really *was* just friends, like a pretty girl being nice to an out-of-town visitor."

Uncle James, who'd been doodling on his yellow pad, looked up sharply. "And then?" he asked. "You kissed her?"

"Well, yes," Steven said. "But it was really just a gentleman-cowboy-to-virtuous-schoolteacher kind of kiss. Only that wasn't what Marissa wanted. 'Gol*lee!*' she said. 'You mean to tell me that's how Yankees kiss?' Or something like that. And she threw her arms around my neck and practically yanked me out of the saddle.

"So I . . . I kissed her. The way she wanted to

be kissed, I guess you could say. Right then an alarm bell went off in my head, all the things y'all—I mean, all of you—warned me about. *She's white*, I was thinking. *Watch out*. But when Marissa led me over to the leather sofa, I followed her."

"And I don't suppose you paid the slightest attention to those alarm bells," Uncle James said with a sigh.

"No," Steven admitted. "I didn't." He looked kind of sheepish. "I was about to kiss Marissa again when I thought I heard a noise. 'What was that?' I asked her and tried to back off. I was feeling pretty nervous about all of this. But Marissa said something like, 'I think it's my heart beating.' She pulled me close and kissed me. Suddenly I sensed somebody looming over us—"

"Jasper!" I exclaimed.

Steven looked at me and nodded. "Right, Em. It was Jasper. Both Marissa and I jumped up, embarrassed, even though we weren't doing anything bad. But what happened next *was* bad. 'So this is what you brought your nigger boyfriend up here for,' Jasper said. 'You ought to be 'shamed of yourself, Marissa.' His exact words.

"I was shocked, him calling me a nigger, and Marissa started crying, just sobbing her heart out. I wanted to grab Jasper by the throat, but I didn't touch him. And I knew that telling him what I thought—that he was nothing but a redneck scumbag—would just make everything worse, so I kept my mouth shut. Then Marissa started to get it together. 'We weren't doing anything wrong,' she told him in a shaky voice. 'He's my friend.'

" 'You want to be friends with his kind, I guess that's your business,' Jasper said. 'I knowed you since you was a little bit of a thing, couldn't even get up on a pony without me helping you. And I think I owe it to your daddy to tell him what you been up to.' There was a telephone on the wall by the bar, and he made a move toward it. 'Maybe I'll just call down there and say hello, let your folks know you and your *friend* got here safe and sound.'

"I figured, let him call, if he wants to. It wasn't like he had caught us . . . *you* know. But Marissa said, 'Jasper, please don't.' I guess my jaw must have dropped about six inches. *Not* call? Why not?

"Then Marissa gives me this feeble smile, kind of apologetic, and right then it was like a light went on: *She hasn't told them about me.* She'd taken me out to her house when her parents weren't home. I hadn't met them. They didn't know anything about me, and I guessed she didn't want them finding out. First I felt hurt; then I got mad. But I kept a lid on it, don't ask me how.

"Jasper put the phone back with this nasty expression on his face. 'I do need one little favor, though.' He eyed me for a few seconds, scratching his chin. 'You wouldn't mind running over to Zippy's in Dinkle, would you, boy, and picking me up some Skoal and, let's see, a six-pack of diet soda, and maybe a couple of those peanut patties?' He reached for his billfold and pulled out a ten-dollar bill. He handed it to me like I had a contagious disease. This didn't make any sense. Why would he be sending me off to get tobacco and candy?"

"And it did not once occur to you that you were being set up?" Uncle James burst in.

Steven shook his head, shamefaced. "No, it didn't. I was so relieved to have an excuse to get out of there, away from this scary jerk, that I jumped at the chance. And Marissa started to come with me.

" 'Uh-uh-uh,' Jasper said, wagging his finger at her. 'Marissa, sweetheart, you're going to stay here. Have a nice glass of iced tea with me and Rita while your boyfriend runs an errand. That would be fine with you, wouldn't it?'

"She nodded, a little too eagerly—like she was on Jasper's side, ganging up against me. I didn't trust this guy, even if Marissa *had* known him practically all her life, and I didn't want to leave her here with him. So I said, 'Not fine, Marissa's coming with me.'

"Jasper took a menacing step toward me. I wondered for a second if I could take him down, if I had to. He's a lot older than me, but tough and hard. I glanced at Marissa. She shook her head no once. Then she told me where the convenience store was. We had passed it coming in. I noticed her voice was shaking.

"So you're right, Uncle James, I didn't get it, and I probably should have. What I still don't know is if Marissa got it, either." Steven stared at his empty glass for what seemed like a long time. "You know what?" he said. "I'm still hungry. Could we take a break and maybe I could get something else to eat? Something not too hard to chew? And then I'll tell the rest of it."

"How about some mocha cake?" Mom said. "We'll all have some. Maybe it will make us feel better." Suddenly there was a flurry. Mom jumped up to serve the cake—the one she wouldn't let me taste because it was for the Sunday picnic—Mother Rose thought a cup of hot tea might be nice, too, and Uncle James wanted to check his answering machine for messages. I stayed at the table with Steven. He really did look awful.

He glanced up at me. "I guess you think I'm pretty stupid," he said.

I thought it over. "Not stupid," I said. "Just extremely naive."

TWENTY-FIVE

The Sheriff

It was close to midnight when Steven resumed his story, but none of us was the least bit sleepy. I could imagine how scared he must have been when he left the ranch for Zippy's, how mad at that insulting jerk Jasper, how disappointed in Marissa for letting him down. But then it got much worse.

"I drove carefully, going forty in a forty-five-mile zone on a stretch of road with nothing but fields on either side," Steven said. "I was tense and scared, but I didn't know of *what* exactly. I just wanted this whole thing to be *over*. I saw the sign for Dinkle, population 240, and then there was Zippy's. An old man was gassing up his Toyota pickup, and there was a couple of beat-up cars parked straight in.

"Inside, the pasty-faced girl behind the checkout counter just glanced at me and then looked away. I found the chewing tobacco, wondering if she'd refuse to sell it to me because I'm underage and I'd find myself in trouble over that. Then I picked up the sodas and candy and handed her Jasper's ten-dollar bill and waited for the change. She put the stuff in a bag and never challenged the tobacco. 'Have a nice day,' she said. She had a yellow smiley-face button pinned to her blouse—I don't know why I noticed *that.* So far so good; it was half over. I thought I'd drive back to the ranch, give Jasper his stuff, pick up Marissa, and get the hell out of there. I was planning all the things I was going to say to her to make her see what she'd done and how bad I felt.

"I didn't see the sheriff's patrol car when I pulled back out onto the county road, but it must have been parked just out of sight around the side of Zippy's. I hadn't gone more than a half mile when I saw the flashing red-and-blue lights in the rearview mirror. I felt sick, but I pulled over and waited for whatever was going to happen."

"Uh-oh," Uncle James said. He laid his glasses on the table and pressed his eyes with the heels of his hands. I guess he could see what was coming.

"Two men in uniform climbed out of the patrol car and walked toward the convertible, in no big hurry. I watched them in the mirror, their hands hovering near their service revolvers. One was in the red zone for overweight, belly hanging over his belt. The younger guy looked in better shape. They both wore dark sunglasses.

" 'Slager County sheriff,' the fat one said, drawling like he had a mouthful of beans. 'Now we want you to move real slow and show us your driver's license.' He studied it for a while, comparing the photograph to my face. 'Connecticut, huh? Lot of you niggers up there?' "

"What did you *say*, Steven?" Mom asked in a voice squeaky with nerves. She was gripping the edge of the table, and I had practically gnawed through my thumb.

"I guess I said, 'Some,' or something like that. I was ready to explode, but I was trying to be superpolite. The younger guy took the license back to the patrol car, while the fat one and I waited, him sweating in the sun, me sitting in the car sweating from pure terror, even though I knew I hadn't done anything wrong. The younger one came back. 'Nothing on the license,' he said, 'but we got a UUV on the beemer.' Then he rattled off something like: You have the right to remain silent, anything you say may be held against you, you have a right to the presence of an attorney, understand?"

"What's a UUV?" I asked.

"Exactly what I wanted to know, Emmy. It means 'Unauthorized Use of Vehicle.' Not quite as bad as stolen, but close."

I knew they'd hush me up if I asked any more questions, but I could not see how anybody would think Steven had taken the car. Then I got it: "*Jasper!*" I yelped. "He called them and lied!"

"You catch on quickly, Emily Rose," Uncle James said. "Go on, Steven."

" 'Real nice car you're driving,' the fat one said. 'You want to tell us where you got ahold of it?' I explained that it belonged to a friend. He made this disgusting smacking sound with his mouth. 'You mind steppin' outta the car, boy?' he asked.

"I got out, never so scared in my life and determined not to show it. 'Keep your hands up where we can see 'em!' I raised my hands over my head. The young guy grabbed me and shoved me against the car. He kicked my feet apart with his boot so that I was spread-eagled over the hood, and he began patting me down. 'Patting' isn't the right word, though, especially not when he checked my testicles.

"The fat one grabbed me and spun me

around. He got his face up to mine, so I could smell his rancid breath. 'We just find it mighty interestin' that a nigger boy like you is driving around in a high-priced luxury car.'

"I explained about Marissa and suggested he look for the registration in the map compartment. The sheriff just hawked and spit in the dust. 'And exactly how does a nigger boy from Connecticut get to be friends with a rich white Texas gal?' When I tried to tell them, they laughed in my face. Then they quit laughing. 'Possible charge of theft here, considering the value of the car. We're taking you in,' the fat one said."

"Lord have mercy," Mother Rose whispered. Mom's mouth was working, but nothing came out. I asked the question for her: "What did you do?"

"I lost it," Steven murmured, his voice so low I could barely make it out. "The whole thing was so outrageous! I yelled some stuff at them, and when they came at me with the handcuffs I tried to fight them off. Stupid, stupid, *stupid*—I know! They both grabbed me, and the young one slapped me, hard, *one-two-three*. One of them knocked my feet out from under me and I sprawled in the dust. I curled in on myself, trying to protect my head with my arms. It didn't work. Nothing worked. The pointed toes of their western boots slammed into my back, my ribs. 'You asked for this, nigger—*you asked for it!*' I heard them yell. I remember vowing I wouldn't scream and then screaming anyway. Then I don't remember much."

Mom had her head in her hands and was crying. Mother Rose had folded her hands on the table in front of her like she was praying. A vein throbbed in Uncle James's forehead. I could barely breathe and wished Dad were here, although I don't know exactly what he would have done.

Steven continued in a matter-of-fact voice. "They cuffed my hands and feet and shoved me face down into the backseat of the sheriff's department car. The fat one drove. The younger one followed in Marissa's car. When we stopped finally the sheriff dragged me inside a building—that courthouse, I guess. I was hurting all over. 'Unauthorized use of vehicle, suspicion of auto theft, resisting arrest,' he told the guy behind the desk. They took mug shots and fingerprints.

"Suddenly the sheriff was all formal and correct. He asked me if I wanted to give a written statement, and I said I did. He took me into the magistrate's office, where a white-haired guy read me my rights again. I wanted to tell this magistrate what the sheriff had done, but I was afraid to. Probably he and the sheriff and Jasper were all buddies, and I'd just get into more trouble.

"Then the sheriff—by now I knew his name was Cates—sat down next to me, like he's my pal, really on my side, and offered to write my statement for me. Not a chance! When I wrote it I tried to explain how Marissa Plunkett and I had gone to visit High Valley Ranch in Marissa's BMW and how the ranch manager, Mr. Jasper, had sent me on a personal errand in the car to Zippy's, where Sheriff Cates had mistakenly assumed I had stolen the car. I crossed out *car* and wrote *vehicle*.

"The magistrate came back and looked over what I had written. Then he asked me a couple of questions, like had I been coerced in any way or had anyone made me any promises if I said certain things. Sure, I'd been coerced! But what was the point? I just wanted to get out of there. I said, 'No, sir' and signed the statement. Then the magistrate told me to call you to come and get me. And that's the end of the story."

"Not exactly," Uncle James said. "You'll get a summons to appear in juvenile court for a hearing. And we may write a chapter or two of our own."

EVERYONE WAS exhausted when Steven finished. Even the "night owl," Mother Rose, looked like a balloon with the air leaking out of it. Then Steven and Mom got into a huge argument about Marissa. He wanted to call her up and after he made sure she had gotten home safely, tell her how upset he was.

"Don't be a total fool, Steven," Mom said. "She really hung you out to dry. *She's* the one who should be calling, to find out what happened to *you*, to find out if *you're* OK. Spoiled little brat!"

"But it really wasn't her fault, Mom," Steven insisted. "She didn't have anything to do with this. It's true she didn't back me up, but she was probably just as upset as I was when I didn't come back and she had no idea what had happened until the sheriff called and told her they had her car. You know they didn't tell her the truth, and who knows what *Jasper* told her! They might have even convinced her that I *had* stolen her car!"

"Steven, dammit, you *are* an idiot!" Mom said. "You've just told us that Marissa was too cowardly to tell her parents about you and that she caved in as soon as Jasper threatened to blow her cover. You wanted to tell her off yourself when you got a chance. You don't owe that girl *anything*!"

"I'd like to suggest," Uncle James broke in wearily, pinching his nose and closing his eyes, "that I agree with Steven, although not for the reasons he cites. It might be a good idea to find out what Dr. and Mrs. Plunkett believe happened. A few words from them to the sheriff's department might have a good effect on how the hearing goes."

"It's too late to call now," Mom protested.

"No, it is not, Susan," Uncle James said calmly. "I believe this qualifies as an emergency. If you prefer, I can make the call for you."

"I'll do it," Mom said. "Emmy, would you see if there's any coffee left in the pot? And then I think you should go to bed."

I fixed her a cup of coffee with boiled milk, the way she likes it, but I ignored her other suggestion. Uncle James said this qualified as an emergency, and I wasn't leaving for anything.

The Plunketts' home phone was unlisted, but Steven had the number for Marissa's separate line. "Let me do it, Mom," Steven said, but Mom said no, it was better if she did it, and Steven didn't argue. Steven, Uncle James, Mother Rose, and I took our places at the kitchen table while Mom dialed the number. We heard her say, "Marissa, this is Susan Chartier, Steven's mother. May I speak to your mother or father, please?" After a pause she added, "He's all right, Marissa, but I do need to speak to one of your parents *right now.*"

Steven covered his face with his hands while Mom explained to Mrs. Plunkett who she was and why she was calling. Then there was another pause while Dr. Plunkett got on the extension phone and Mom introduced herself again, this time going all the way back to when Catherine Jane Bell and Rose Lee Jefferson played together as children on down through Rose Lee taking care of Catherine Jane's son, Tommy, who was Dr. Plunkett's father.

"That's right, that's *right*," Mother Rose muttered, and Uncle James put his finger to his lips, signaling her to whisper.

Then Mom moved into how the Plunketts' daughter Marissa had gotten Mother Rose's great-grandson Steven into deep, *deep* trouble for allegedly stealing Marissa's car. We couldn't hear what Mrs. Plunkett was saying, but whatever it was was making Mom furious.

"It's no wonder she's not feeling well this evening," Mom said impatiently. "Do you know where your daughter was all day?" She plunged ahead, explaining exactly what had happened to Steven. "My son has been beaten and humiliated and dragged off to jail. He's being charged with unauthorized use of a vehicle and resisting arrest. He's here with me now, but he'll have to go to a hearing and might even have to do time in jail unless you *do* something." Then Mom kind of ran out of steam. "Please," she begged. "Maybe our kids have been foolish, but my son is paying too high a price for it. Please help us!" Whatever Mrs. Plunkett had to say to that, I don't know. Mom listened. "All right," she said, and listened again. "Yes. All right."

At last she hung up and turned to Steven. "Dr. Plunkett says he'll contact the sheriff and explain that it was all a misunderstanding. But you're not to have anything further to do with Marissa. That's the price. Understand?"

Steven nodded grimly. "Did they say how Marissa got her car back? How she got home?"

"They did not. Apparently it wasn't a problem."

"They need to fire that Jasper fella, that's what they need to do," Mother Rose said. "But they won't. Now it's time for us all to go to bed." Uncle James helped her to her feet. "Things always look better in daylight. Besides, tomorrow is the Lord's day."

TWENTY-SIX

Sunday

THINGS DIDN'T LOOK any better on the Lord's day.

I didn't sleep much. What had happened to Steven happened because Steven is black. Here in Dillon being double didn't mean a thing. Being double was something that existed only in our heads. No wonder Brandy jeered at me when I said I was *double. I am also black!* Finally I understood clearly that those two aren't the same thing at all.

Mom didn't sleep much, either. I know, because she tossed and turned next to me all night, and her eyes looked puffy in the morning. Uncle James was the only one up and busy, getting on with the day. He always fixed a big breakfast on Sunday, he informed us: eggs and sausage and grits and biscuits and gravy. Mom ate hardly anything, but Steven ate like a starving man.

Then Robby came home from Nathan's house, where he'd spent the night. Word was already out that something was going on, and the rumors had reached Nathan's. "His mom and dad said Mom and Uncle James left before the party even got started and never came back," Robby reported. "They figured Uncle James got a call, and they were all wondering who could have died." Then he got a look at Steven's face. "What happened?" he asked, wide-eyed.

"Nobody died," Steven said. "I got in some trouble with the sheriff, is all. It's OK. Don't worry about it."

But Robby is not dumb. One look at the long, tired faces around the breakfast table, and he wasn't buying that "don't worry" stuff.

Then Brandy called me. "How come your momma left so early last night?" she wanted to know. "Hardly anybody got a look at Auntie Lu'Rae's red robe before she was gone. Just disappeared, they said. Mr. Dilworth, who took your uncle James's place as master of ceremonies, he said there was a family emergency but he didn't say *what*, and that got everybody so curious they hardly listened to anything he had to say after that. So what happened?"

I didn't like the idea of everybody in Southeast knowing all about this business, but I guess it was pretty stupid of me to think it could turn out any other way. I've never been any good about "avoiding the truth," as my dad calls it. "Steven got arrested," I said, and gave her a short version of my brother's troubles. I didn't want to tell her about Marissa, but without Marissa there wouldn't have been a story. When I finished, Brandy skipped right over Jasper and the sheriff, who I thought were the real villains, and zoomed in on Marissa.

"*Oooooh!*" Brandy shrieked. "Wouldn't I just like to slap her *ugly* face! Maybe this will teach him to quit messing around with white girls."

I hated it that she was right. "Don't gloat," I said. "Everybody makes mistakes, Brandy. Even you, I bet."

"I'm not gloating, but you got to admit it was a dumb thing he did." Then she added, "I gotta go. See you in church, Emily Rose."

I'd forgotten about church. "Are we going to mass?" I asked Mom after I'd hung up.

She shook her head. "Not today," she said. "We're going with Mother Rose. This is part of the Juneteenth Jubilee."

"It's a good thing to have church this morning," Mother Rose said. "You'll be lifted up." She was already dressed in her navy blue dress with the white collar, her black straw hat perched on her nest of gray hair, her shiny black pocketbook clutched in both hands.

The problem was to get Steven looking as though he hadn't been run over by a truck. He protested, but Mom put a little makeup around his swollen eye to try to camouflage it. The cut on his lip was too obvious to conceal.

We sat in the same pew as on Wednesday night, and Brandy was in her same seat in the choir, grinning at me and shooting sharp looks at Steven, too. I was sure she was gloating, no matter what she said. The service lasted all morning. Mother Rose was right, it was good for us. You could not sit through that service without being lifted up.

When Mr. Phillips played the piano, you could not help tapping your foot. Sometimes everybody sang, and the choir did some special numbers. Pastor Hilton knelt beside the pulpit and prayed in his lilting Jamaican accent. It was while he was praying that I had a sudden inspiration: *Wouldn't it be great if Mother Rose would let us bring her paintings here to the church and have them on display for her talk on Tuesday evening!* The more I thought about it, the more excited I got. Now I just had to think of a way to convince her.

People stood up and introduced relatives

visiting for the Juneteenth Jubilee. There were more announcements about plans for the climax of the celebration on Wednesday night. Then Pastor Hilton introduced Pastor Freedom Gibbons from Kansas City. "Cousin Cora's boy," Mother Rose reminded me in a loud whisper.

Pastor Gibbons was a small man with dark wrinkled skin and snow white hair that stood out like a fluffy cloud around his head. He clasped his hands beneath his chin and peered out at the congregation.

"Let's hear it, brother," Mother Rose said clearly.

Pastor Gibbons opened a Bible with worn leather covers and laid it on the pulpit. "The story of Daniel," he said.

Yesssss, the congregation breathed.

Then Pastor Gibbons told the story of King Nebuchadnezzar getting into a rage and throwing three Israelites, Shadrach, Meshach, and Abednego, into the fiery furnace and how the fire never touched them because an angel protected them. And how Nebuchadnezzar's son, King Belshazzar, had Daniel thrown into a den full of lions, but Daniel came out without a single scratch.

It was just a short jump for Pastor Gibbons from that story in the Bible to the story of how the people of Freedomtown had been tested seventy-five years ago when their community was destroyed and their homes taken away, and how the people of Greenville and other places in the South are still being tested when their churches are burned. Back and forth he went, the wicked king and Daniel with his faith in God on the one hand, and on the other what the people of Freedomtown endured and lots of black people continue to endure. I glanced over at Steven, who was keeping his head down. I thought if Pastor Gibbons knew about what happened to my brother, he could have put that in his sermon, too.

All the while Pastor Gibbons was preaching, people in the congregation were talking back at him. "Amen!" they said. "Tell it, brother! Hallelujah!" The more they shouted their approval, the more wound up the preacher got. He paced back and forth, playing first the part of the fierce king and then of brave Daniel. He even played the roaring lions waiting to pounce on Daniel. Pastor Gibbons's wrinkled old face was shiny with sweat.

At last he began to wind down. "Amen," he said softly.

"Amen, amen," the congregation murmured, and I added my voice: "Amen."

Then the choir was on their feet, swaying and clapping, and Mr. Phillips was ripping up and down the keyboard with thunderous chords, and the choir began to sing until everybody in the congregation was on their feet, swaying and clapping. A single soprano voice soared and then seemed to float above everyone else's—*like an angel*, I thought, as shivers ran up my spine. It was Brandy. That made me laugh, because if there's one thing Brandy is not, it's an angel.

The service ended with everybody singing, "We Shall Overcome," and we left the church singing, following the choir right out the front door of the church. I did feel uplifted.

Pastor Gibbons and Pastor Hilton led the procession, followed by the choir, still wearing their royal blue choir robes with the gold satin stoles around their necks, FORGIVENESS embroidered down one side and PRAISE THE LORD down the other. The rest of us fell in behind them, trying to keep up with the words to the song.

Mother Rose took my arm and held it tight as we walked. "Keep singing, Emily Rose," she said when I kind of let it slide, thinking this might be a good time to mention the paintings. But that would have to wait; right now I had to sing.

We marched to Martin Luther King Jr. Park, a few blocks from the church. Quite a few other people were gathering in the big tents. Long tables covered with red-and-white checkered tablecloths were heaped with food. Uncle James had already delivered our contribution—what looked to me like enough fried chicken to feed the whole congregation. People from Mt. Olive AME Church had set up a smoker, a huge black oven, and were serving barbecued ribs. One table was crowded with nothing but desserts, pies, cakes, and cobblers. (The mocha cake was not there; Steven and I had demolished a big part of it the night before.) The Forgiveness choir was in charge of dishing up ice cream.

I had just finished my fourth fried chicken wing—my favorite part of the bird—when Nathan's parents came by to say hello and told Mom how much they enjoyed having Robby over to visit. Meanwhile on the temporary stage at one end of the park, Mr. Phillips tipped up the lid on an upright piano. He started off with a few little ripples and runs, and then he tore into some ragtime, stomping his foot to keep time. Pretty soon he had everybody clapping and stomping right along with him.

It wasn't only that kind of fun, though, because there had to be some solemn speeches. Pastors from each of the black churches got up and said "a few words" that turned out to be very long-winded. I saw Mother Rose start to nod off. In between there were musical offerings:

A gospel quartet was the most popular with the older people—it woke Mother Rose up again—and there was a Christian rapper from the "new church" (twenty-five years at their location out on the highway, Mother Rose explained) who went over big with the young people.

I loved being part of all of it—the family, the church, the celebration. There was nothing like this back home in Northdale. *I wish I could stay*, I thought. *Not forever—just for a while*.

The day would have been perfect if hadn't been for Steven's trouble. All afternoon word about what had happened to him spread through that big crowd of hundreds of people like an epidemic of chicken pox. People we didn't even know came over to ask how it was going. There was a lot of upset talk about the Slager County sheriff's reputation. Some people suggested that Mom ought to bring charges against the sheriff's department, or sue the Plunketts and do something bad to Jasper. Mom was polite to everybody, but I knew she'd never do anything like that.

Brandy strolled over carrying a bowl of ice cream, which she set down in front of Steven. "Hey," she said, "I'm Brandy. Somebody told me you had a bad time last night."

What nerve! I thought. Brandy sure had it. I envied her.

Steven managed a lopsided smile. "Yeah," he said, digging into the ice cream, "I did." I knew that Steven was horribly embarrassed by the fuss and wished it would all go away, but he was trying to act good humored.

"I heard you singing in church, Brandy," I said, to change the subject. "You've got a great voice."

"Lovely," my mother said.

"Yes, indeed," Mother Rose agreed, "real nice."

Then Auntie Lu'Rae came by, and Mom got a chance to thank her in person for the loan of the red robe—"the most magnificent thing I've ever worn in my life," Mom said, "and I didn't get much chance to show it off. I guess you heard that your robe didn't stay long at the ball," she added.

"I couldn't believe it when I saw Mom walk into the jail in that outfit," Steven said, perking up a little. "And Uncle James in a white tuxedo!"

Auntie Lu'Rae laughed, but then she got serious. "When you're up in Slager County, best remember what they say," she advised Steven. " 'You black, git back.' And that's *especially* true if you're young and happen to be male." She gave him a hug that must have hurt.

"I got to go help out at the ice-cream table,"

Brandy said, getting up to leave. "Come on over if you want to, Emily Rose."

I was thinking of going with Brandy when Marcus Overton arrived at our table and introduced himself to Mom. I decided to stick around. Mom offered her condolences for the passing of Cornelius, and Marcus said things like, "He lived a full life. He'll be missed." I glanced over at Mother Rose, who was sitting up straight and stiff as a tree.

Then Marcus Overton got down to business. "May I?" he asked, indicating that he wanted to sit down on the bench next to Mom. She scooted over to make room for him—Marcus is not a skinny man. "James tells me you've had some trouble," he said. "With the law," he added, nodding toward Steven.

"Yes," Mom said carefully. "But I think it's going to work out all right."

"I'm an attorney," he said. "I would be happy to represent your son at his hearing. And to help in any other way I can."

"The Plunketts said they'd make sure the charges are dropped."

"Charges of auto theft or UUV, possibly. But there may be nothing they can do about the charge of resisting arrest." He handed Mom his business card. "I'm offering my services *gratis*," Marcus said.

"Thank you very much for your offer. I'm just anxious to get Steven home," Mom said, slipping the card into her purse.

"When do you plan to leave?"

"Thursday, the day after Juneteenth."

"You *are* an optimist, aren't you," Marcus said, and raised his bushy eyebrows. "Will you let me help you?" he asked. "I'll contact Dr. Plunkett and make sure he understands what's at stake. Have you taken your son to a doctor?" Mom shook her head. "Then I suggest you do that, and get these injuries documented. There's a clinic not far from here. Also, buy a little disposable camera and take some photographs—for the record. Meanwhile, I may do a little snooping around and find out what I can about this Mr. Jasper at High Valley Ranch and what the relationship is between him and Sheriff Cates. Apply a little pressure here and there." He smiled, stood up, and shook Mom's hand. "Don't worry," he said, and smiled at Steven. "It's going to be fine."

We watched him walk away, and I sneaked another look at Mother Rose. She was no longer just a tree; she had turned to stone. "I never thought the day would come," she said, "when I'd be accepting help from an Overton."

"I'm sorry, Mother Rose," Mom said. "I never intended for us to cause you any trouble." She attempted a smile. "A few more days and we'll be gone."

"I know," Mother Rose whispered, and she pushed up her glasses and wiped her eyes.

I counted it out on my fingers: We'd been in Dillon five days already. In four days we'd be back on the bus again, heading northeast—unless something bad happened with Steven that Marcus Overton couldn't fix. And although I didn't want anything bad to happen to Steven, I really, *really* wished I had more than just four days left in Dillon. *Maybe a few more weeks*, I thought. *Maybe the rest of the summer*.

TWENTY-SEVEN

Exhibition

STEVEN LOOKED even worse on Monday. The cuts were healing and the swelling was down some, but he had purple bruises everywhere. Mom went out and got a camera first thing. Right after breakfast she snapped pictures of the ugly marks on his back and ribs where he'd been kicked. It made me furious to look at them and think of the horrible people who had done this to my brother. Then, even though there was a phone right there in the kitchen, Mom went into Uncle James's office to call Dad. When she came out, I could tell she'd been crying, but before I could say anything she hurried Steven out the door to drive him to the clinic for a medical report.

Later in the morning Marcus Overton

appeared, and while Mother Rose sat at the table looking as though she had swallowed ground glass, Mom and Steven left with Marcus to drive up to Slagerville to visit the sheriff. I didn't ask to go along this time. I had a plan that had nothing to do with Steven: I wanted to tell Mother Rose about my inspiration and persuade her to let us hang her paintings in the church for Tuesday evening.

But first I had to give her time to blow off a little steam at the Overtons in general and at Marcus in particular, even though Marcus was helping us out. "What about Brandy?" I asked when she was done. "You said she has a good heart. Marcus is her uncle."

Mother Rose thought it over. "Yes, she does," she said finally. Then she added sternly, "But never forget, Emily Rose, that she is an Overton."

Finally I eased into the subject of exhibiting her paintings at the church. At first she said no. "I've never been a show-off," Mother Rose said disapprovingly.

"But this isn't showing off," I said. "It's *sharing*. I think your pictures would mean a lot to people. Besides," I added, "I got the inspiration when I was listening to Pastor Hilton praying yesterday."

"You don't say," Mother Rose said. "While he was praying?"

"Yes," I said. "That's the truth. I wouldn't swear it was the prayer that did it, but I wouldn't swear it *wasn't*. Please, Mother Rose!"

She looked at me thoughtfully. "All right, Emily Rose," she said. "I'm doing this for you. I'll call Pastor Hilton and see if he'd like to borrow them."

I hugged her excitedly. "I can take them down and wrap them," I said. "Then I'll ask Mr. Phillips to drive them to the church in the van."

Later, when I was carrying the paintings, wrapped in old sheets, out to the van, Brandy showed up. "What's this stuff?" she asked.

"Pictures," I said, giving her a short answer and figuring she could see for herself when we got them to the church. She grabbed a couple and stacked them in the van. "How's Steven?" she asked. That's what she was *really* interested in.

"He's gone with Mom and your uncle Marcus to see the sheriff," I said. "I wish we could do something really *bad* to that sheriff," I admitted, "so he never treats anybody that way again."

"Huh! Nothing you can do to a redneck honky SOB like that," Brandy said, flashing anger.

I was glad Mom wasn't around to hear Brandy's language. Mom always told us not to call names, but a man who was supposed to be respected and then acted the way the sheriff did toward my brother really *was* a redneck honky SOB and, in my opinion, deserved to be called just about anything you could think of. Sheriff Cates was right up there with King Nebuchadnezzar as somebody who could make your life miserable because he had all the power, and you had none. Brandy and I had a good time coming up with foul names for the sheriff while we loaded the van.

Mr. Phillips drove Brandy and me and the paintings over to Forgiveness. Then he had to hurry back; there had been another call, and he and Uncle James had to go pick up a dead body. Mother Rose was tired and had decided not to come along with us. "Whatever you want to do is fine with me, Emily Rose," she'd said.

Pastor Hilton seemed completely amazed when we carried in those paintings and took the sheets off. "What a treasure!" he exclaimed. "Praise the Lord and give thanks to Him for the talent He's bestowed upon that remarkable woman."

Even Brandy seemed impressed. "Who are all those people?" she wanted to know.

"I'll explain while we're hanging them."

Treasure or not, though, Pastor Hilton wasn't

about to let anybody go around putting nail holes in the wood-paneled walls of his church where I wanted to hang them. My idea was that people could be looking at the pictures while Mother Rose talked about how Freedomtown was when she was a girl. He told us we could prop the paintings up on a row of folding metal chairs he'd bring in from the Sunday school room.

I had spent a lot of time studying those paintings and listening to Mother Rose's stories about them. While Brandy and I waited for Pastor Hilton to come back, I told her as much as I could remember about each picture. She was politely interested until I got to the one showing empty-hearted Cornelius Overton.

"My great-grandpa was in love with your great-grandma?" Brandy asked incredulously. "No foolin'? You bein' straight with me? Hey, we could've ended up sisters!" That idea struck her as hilarious. I thought it was pretty funny, too. "Listen," Brandy said, between fits of laughter, "I'm going to let you in on a secret, Emily Rose." She put her mouth close to my ear and whispered, "Mother Rose was right."

I pulled back and looked at her. "Right?"

"Not to marry Cornelius. I know what all they've been saying about him since he died, but that man was *mean*! When my momma and daddy got divorced, Corny said it was all Momma's fault, and she shouldn't come to him for help. Momma told him she didn't need his help. There were some bad feelings there."

Well, well, well, I thought. *So Mother Rose wasn't the only one who didn't like him.* But I didn't want to hurt Brandy's feelings any more about her parents' divorce, so I just mumbled, "Too bad he was like that."

Then the pastor brought the chairs, and no more was said about Cornelius while Brandy and I set up the chairs and arranged the pictures, propping them up with hymn books. I showed her the painting of Aunt Susannah and told her the story of Henry's escape.

"I'll say this for you, Emily Rose," Brandy said admiringly, "you probably know a lot more about Old Freedomtown than most people in Southeast. Trouble is, you still don't know *squat* about what it's like living here now!"

I hated to admit she was right. "Not much I can do about *that,*" I said.

"When y'all going back to Connecticut?" Brandy asked after a bit.

"Thursday," I said. "It takes two whole days to get there, and Mom has to open up her restaurant on Monday."

"Y'all come down here for what?—a week, ten days? And then you get on the bus and go home, and what have you learned about being a black person here *today*? Zip! Exactly nothin'! Am I right?"

"Uh-huh," I said.

"You ought to stick around here awhile," Brandy advised. "Bet if you did, I could teach you a whole lot you're not learning about up there in Connecticut. You'd quit thinking, 'I'm not a little ol' nigger like you.' You're so busy being 'double' this and 'double' that, you aren't bothering to find out about the *single* part of you. You're going to tell me you know all about the fur trappers or whoever that came over here from France on your daddy's side. But I'm telling *you*, you don't know the first *thing* about being black. Hang with me, and you'd cut out that 'French American African American' crap real quick! I'd get you some *pride*, you know what I'm sayin'?"

"Whoa!" I said. "Hold it right there, Brandy! Because you don't have the least idea what I'm thinking! You just *think* you do. The reason my mother brought us down here was just exactly so we'd find out about the 'single part,' the black part. Not to get rid of the white part, even if you think I should! I didn't know that was why we were coming, but I know it now. I bet I've learned more about my family and myself in the last five days than you've learned about yours in your whole life. So you, Brandy, are the one who'd better cut the crap."

Now I was glad my mother wasn't around to hear *my* language—she doesn't approve of me using the word *crap*—but I was pretty sure she'd cheer for the way I was standing up to Brandy.

Brandy stared at me. "We're fighting again," she said.

"Looks that way."

"I better go."

"Me, too."

We told Pastor Hilton that we were finished, and we left the church. "You know where I'd start?" Brandy asked after a long silence as we walked along.

"Start what?"

"On you. You've learned a lot, like you say, but you still got a ways to go."

"Brandy, just drop it!" I yelled.

"No, no, no, don't get upset," she said calmly, although I already was. "I'd start with that fine white-girl hair you got."

My hands flew up to cover my head. "What do you want to do to my hair?"

"Do you some braids," she said.

"Braids? Like yours?"

"Wouldn't even have to add on any Kanekalon, I bet."

"Add on what?"

"The fake stuff. You saw Auntie Lu'Rae using it the other day on Rhonda. You don't think this is all *real*, do you?" She swung one of her braids around in front to give me a better look at it. "Shoot, there's about a couple pounds of fake stuff braided onto my own." She tossed her head and whipped the braids around like ropes. "I could do them for you tomorrow. I'll get my cousin Ta Lula to help me. She's real good at it. Even so, it'll take pretty near the whole day. Then you'll have them for Mother Rose's night at the church."

I loved Brandy's braids, and I was beginning to like the idea of having some myself even if it meant having someone touch my hair. "Yeah," I said, "I want you to do me some braids."

"Now you're talkin'! Soundin' more like me all the time! We'll start right after breakfast. And I meant what I said about you staying here for the rest of the summer. Ta Lula and me and some of my friends—I bet we could make you into a sister, for sure. You think about it, Emily Rose."

I didn't tell her I already *was* thinking about it. Brandy didn't need to know everything.

TWENTY-EIGHT

Braids

BRANDY AND TA LULA worked on me for nine hours, which was awful. They wouldn't let me look in the mirror that whole time. "You can see it when we're done," Brandy said. I could hardly stand it, wondering what I looked like.

I couldn't believe it took them so long to do my braids. And that was with Auntie Lu'Rae supervising, making sure they sectioned my hair into little boxes and started the braid close enough to my scalp so it wouldn't hang down all droopy, but also not pulling it so tight it yanked the hair right out of my head.

"Sugar, if I was doing it for you," Auntie Lu'Rae said, "I could do it by myself in eight hours, but these two are slow, you know, because they're not professionals. They just do it for fun. Still, you are going to look so *good* when they're done with you!"

While they worked on me, Brandy and Ta Lula talked and joked about people they knew and I didn't. That gave me plenty of time to think about what Brandy had said—that I didn't have a clue about what it was like to live with black people. I knew she was right, and that hurt, because it made it seem like my parents had been doing something wrong, bringing us up as doubles. "You shouldn't have to choose," Mom had said. "Because if you choose to be one, then that means you're rejecting the other."

Even before Brandy suggested it, I'd been thinking about asking Mom if I could stay in Dillon for a few more weeks. So far I hadn't mentioned it. I didn't know how she'd react. I didn't even know how *I* would react! It wasn't just giving up my plans to be a junior curator at the nature center. It would mean being away from my mom and dad and my brothers—well, maybe I wouldn't miss my brothers so much—and I'd never been away from them for more than a couple of days. It also meant staying by myself with Mother Rose and Uncle James, and they are both so old. Then there was Brandy and her determination to make me a blacker person than I already am, and *that* was the scariest thing of all.

Do I want to be black like Brandy? Or do I want to keep on being a double, mixed race, half-breed—whatever you want to call it? That was my dilemma, and I couldn't make up my mind.

Meanwhile, the conversation above my head worked its way back to Steven and his troubles at High Valley Ranch.

"Can't believe that Steven was so *dumb*," Brandy was saying. "You saw him at church, Ta Lula," Brandy told her cousin. "This brother looks exactly like Denzel Washington, but he doesn't have the brains not to go out with white girls. Gets you in trouble every time. Maybe he's learned his lesson now."

"Steven is not dumb!" I insisted. "He's gone out with white girls before. How was he supposed to know he was walking into a trap? He trusted Marissa, because he thought they were friends. Maybe it's different down here, but my brothers and I were raised to believe that friendship doesn't depend on the color of a person's skin. Maybe that's a lesson *you* have to learn!"

Ta Lula burst out laughing. "Finally, somebody stands up to you, Brandy!" She thumped my shoulder. "Good for you, Emily Rose."

"*Whoo-eee!*" Brandy chortled. She yanked on

a braid. "Better watch your mouth, Emily Rose, or I'll quit and leave you half done."

Then at last the torture was over, and I was allowed to see the results. I hardly recognized myself. Auntie Lu'Rae came running out with a camera and took my picture. Then she snapped pictures of me with Brandy and Ta Lula. I looked like an entirely different person—a whole new Emily Rose.

I WAS COMPLETELY pumped up as I hit the back door, barely in time for dinner. But I had forgotten that Freedom Gibbons would be there. They were just sitting down at the table when I made my grand entrance. Everybody stopped talking and stared.

"My God," Mom breathed. There were a lot of *my*, *my*, *mys* from Uncle James and Mother Rose and Pastor Gibbons. "You look like a rap star," said Robby seriously, and Steven applauded.

"I got it done for tonight," I said. I filled my plate with barbecued beef and sat down. "What happened with the sheriff?" I asked Steven, trying to steer the subject away from my hair.

"It went pretty well. Dr. Plunkett showed up, too. He's not that bad of a guy—he was pretty upset, I guess. And he and Marcus persuaded the sheriff to drop the charges, even the resisting arrest charge after Mom showed them the photographs." He smiled, and I noticed for the first time that his front tooth had been chipped. "I'm a free man."

After a while they forgot about me and my hair, and Freedom Gibbons and Uncle James got into a discussion over who had the best barbecue, Dillon or Kansas City. It was heating up to an argument when Robby interrupted. "I want to hear more about Daniel and those three other guys," he said, and that made everybody laugh.

"Those guys," Pastor Gibbons said, "were called Shadrach, Meshach, and Abednego." Then he made Robby and Steven and me practice saying that until we got it right. "Don't they teach you that in Sunday School?" Pastor Gibbons wanted to know.

"Not in ours," Robby said. "We're Catholic."

That got us into the subject of Mom and Dad's mixed marriage. "Baptist and Catholic, black and white, all are precious in His sight," Mom said lightly, repeating a rhyme she'd taught us when we were little. Freedom Gibbons frowned. Mom's shoulders stiffened. I bit my thumb.

"Now what about that nice cobbler you put in the oven, James?" Mother Rose asked.

Uncle James hurried to get the dessert. "Shouldn't be any argument at all about where the best peach cobbler comes from," he said, and the tense moment passed.

Then it was time to get ready for "An Evening with Mother Rose."

I FELT EXTREMELY self-conscious when we arrived at Forgiveness Baptist Church for Mother Rose's talk, wondering if people would think I had gone crazy to get this hairstyle. The funny thing is, some people didn't even seem to notice. And the others thought I looked great.

Brandy took all the credit. "Don't you just love it?" she kept asking people. "It was my idea, and Ta Lula and I did it, isn't that right, Emily Rose?"

Not everybody was paying attention to my braids. Most of them were examining Mother Rose's paintings. I wondered if anybody would recognize the one of Cornelius Overton.

Mother Rose made her way slowly to the front of the church and sat in a big wooden armchair that had been put there for her and draped with a beautiful purple cloth. Pastor Hicks introduced her, saying that of course the oldest living survivor of Old Freedomtown needed no introduction and then talking for another ten minutes about her.

She nodded and thanked him, and then she thanked me, "Emily Rose Chartier, only daughter of the only daughter of my only daughter, whose idea it was to bring all these poor little pictures over from my room, to share them with you tonight." I was embarrassed, but it was also nice to have everyone clap.

The crowded church for once was absolutely quiet so as not to miss a word she had to say. "I remember a Juneteenth night so long ago," she began in her soft voice, "when the Klan paid a visit to Freedomtown. Hundreds of hooded figures, but no sound at all but the *tramp tramp tramp* of their feet as they passed our house, on their way to Forgiveness Baptist Church. From where I hid I could see one of them plant a big wooden cross in the ground and set it alight. 'Remember this, niggers!' one of them yelled. And I always have remembered, and will to my dying day."

I shivered as I listened to that story.

After she had reminisced about other times in Old Freedomtown, some good and some bad, Mother Rose said, "Now all of that is long over, but that doesn't mean we should forget it! Oh, no! We must never forget our past. We must remember all that has gone before—the good *and* the bad—and celebrate it. That's what makes our community strong."

"Amen," we said. "Amen! Hallelujah!"

There was not to be any choir singing that

evening, no music was planned, but somewhere in the back of the church a voice began humming, and pretty soon others joined in humming as well. Then the humming turned into singing that grew louder—"Amazing Grace." I could hear Brandy's voice sailing above everybody else's. She might have been the one who started it.

LATER, MOM AND I lay side by side in the yellow bedroom.

"Hard to believe tomorrow's our last day in Dillon," she said with a sigh.

Suddenly I knew, clearly and without a single doubt: *I want to stay*. Not to be more like Brandy, though—to be more like *me*, whatever that turns out to be. What I didn't know was exactly how to explain that to Mom, but I had to try.

"Mom?" I began. "What would you think if I said I'd like to stay longer? Maybe for the rest of the summer?"

Mom didn't answer right away. I was afraid she was going to say no. But instead she asked, "*Why* do you want to stay, Emmy?"

"Because there are so many things I want to learn here," I answered. "That I *need* to learn. Not just from Mother Rose, but from Uncle James and Brandy and Auntie Lu'Rae and Ta

Lula and maybe Marcus Overton and all the rest."

Still no answer. I could hear my mother's quiet breathing. "Mom," I said, "I have to learn what it means to be black. Or I'll never really understand what it means to be *me*."

She reached for my hand. "All this time I was so worried about what it was going to be like for me to come home again," she said slowly, "that I didn't really understand what it would mean to you. And so I'd say it's a very, very good idea, Emily Rose. We'll work out the details in the morning, but right now, I'm going to sleep."

"Thank you," I whispered. Mom squeezed my hand and rolled over. I lay awake for a long time, feeling the strangeness of my new braids, and singing "Amazing Grace" in my head.

TWENTY-NINE

Jubilee

I KNEW I'd made the right decision to stay when we all gathered on Juneteenth in the Great Hall of the college. Mother Rose's pictures hung in the lobby by the main entrance, brought over from the church by a committee of admirers who thought everybody should see them. Brandy sang with the choir in her blue-and-gold robe and then later reappeared in black-and-white striped shortalls to perform with the Uptown Girls, her R & B group from school. Mother Rose's white friend Phoebe Kingsley came to sit with us, and we were all introduced and exclaimed over.

There were, of course, speeches—too many, to my thinking. The mayor of Dillon, who is white, had something to say—I don't remember what. I wasn't paying much attention. But I did pay attention to the president of the Dillon Community College, Dr. Evelyn Lake, a black woman with her hair cropped very short. I hoped Brandy wouldn't get any ideas about doing that to me! Dr. Lake talked about the history of the college from the time it was a school for white girls that had been a major force in getting rid of Freedomtown back in the 1920s. Today the school has lots of African American students. Some of the black alumni were on the platform, too.

Next came the two black members of the Dillon City Council, including Marcus Overton, who merely stood up, waved, and sat down again.

Then Pastor Hilton rose and strode to the podium. "Let me read to you from the twenty-fifth chapter of Leviticus," he boomed, and I got ready not to listen. But then I perked up a little bit, because I could feel everybody else paying close attention: He was telling us how the Bible described a jubilee.

The way Pastor Hilton explained it, the ancient Hebrews had a custom that every fifty years was a jubilee year. It was a year that caused wonderful things to happen: "In the year of this jubilee ye shall return every man unto his possession." Not only that, said Pastor Hilton, it was the year in which slaves were to be set free. That was why there were so many old hymns and spirituals that sang about the jubilee. In modern times, he added, every twenty-five years was often called a jubilee.

"How appropriate, then," Pastor Hilton boomed, "that at this seventy-fifth jubilee observance of the end of Freedomtown, this community now has received this wonderful message, that the time has come for one of *our* possessions to be returned. It has been suggested, perhaps by a messenger from on high, that the old Ragsdale home be brought back, salvaged from ruination and decay, and restored to its former beauty. It would, I think, make a splendid place in which to hang—if the artist agrees—this wonderful collection of paintings of Freedomtown. White Dillon has its Bell Mansion; African American Dillon would have Ragsdale House. What say you? Is this not a poss-i-bil-i-ty?" he asked, turning to the mayor and council members.

The white mayor blinked, as though he didn't have the least idea what was going on. But Marcus Overton rose, stepped to the microphone, and said smoothly, "I have already taken the liberty of calling for the formation of a committee to study this excellent suggestion and to make a proposal."

Mother Rose was almost ready to jump out of her skin, and I poked Steven, the "messenger from on high," with my elbow.

There were a few more speeches, not too many and not too long, and then we all stood and joined hands and sang "Lift Every Voice and Sing," sometimes called the Black National Anthem. Suddenly I felt embarrassed: I'd learned "We Shall Overcome" in our music class at school in the unit on Songs of Liberation and Protest, but I'd never sung the Black National Anthem before, because I'd never been in a big auditorium filled with mostly black people. I hoped no one noticed I had to read the words from the program, where they were printed for the benefit of visitors from the white community who didn't know them, either. I kept the program, so I'd be sure to memorize the words. Another example that Brandy was right—I had so much to learn!

After the speeches there was a big party. In the rotunda of the new library, tables had been set up with refreshments—iced tea and lemonade and cookies and a huge cake with JUNETEENTH JUBILEE FREEDOMTOWN 1921–1996 spelled out in pink-and-green letters on the chocolate icing. A band played outside on the patio.

I got some food and was looking around for

somebody I knew when I found Steven, surrounded by a crowd of Uptown Girls. There was Brandy, several inches taller than any of the others.

"Hey, Emily Rose!" she called when she saw me. "A bunch of us are going over to Sharonda's for a party. Y'all come, too." She grinned at me. "Steven's gonna come, right, Steven?"

Steven shook his head. "Thanks, but I'll say no. My mom and my brother and I are leaving tomorrow." He draped his arm around my shoulders. "I'm sticking with Emily Rose for the rest of the evening," he said. "I guess you know she's staying here."

Brandy let out an ecstatic whoop and snatched me away from Steven in a wild Brandy-style hug.

THERE WAS a whole lot more hugging when the Greyhound bus pulled into Dillon on Thursday morning, but nobody was ecstatic. I had to swallow hard when Mom and Steven and Robby climbed aboard, and Mother Rose and Uncle James and I waited until they had found seats and smiled out the window at us. Mom was crying and not even pretending she wasn't. Mother Rose stood close beside me, holding my hand, as the bus pulled away. We waved and waved

Just when I felt an ocean of homesickness crash over me and thought I was going to drown in tears, Mother Rose said, "All through life, people we love come and go. Now let's go home, Emily Rose. I have something special to show you."

We climbed into Uncle James's Lincoln—I sat alone in the backseat, feeling lonely but excited, too—and drove back to the funeral parlor. I followed Mother Rose to her bedroom, which seemed eerily empty now with the walls completely bare. But I saw that another canvas was propped on the easel, turned to the wall.

"I thought I'd have this further along by now," she said, "but it's been such a busy few days, I've had hardly any time to work on it. And I've been getting so tired lately!" She laid her hand over her heart, and I couldn't help noticing how frail she looked.

I helped her turn the easel and stepped back to look at the half-finished painting of four young girls. The background was blank, but the features of each face were clear. "It's a family portrait," she explained. "Me on the left when I was a girl, and next is Emily when *she* was a girl, and then your momma, and then you, Emily Rose. I'm sure to have it done by the time you leave. We both have so much to accomplish this summer! It's to be a gift for you, so you'll always remember."

I gazed at the four of us joined by the blood in our veins, the only daughter of the only daughter of the only daughter of Mother Rose. "Of course I'll always remember," I promised.

In the painting I'm the one with my hair in braids.

DILLON REGISTER

Wednesday, January 29, 1997

Rose Lee Jefferson Mobley, known to local residents as Mother Rose, died in her sleep on Tuesday, January 28. She was 87 years old.

Mrs. Mobley, widow of the late Reverend Edmund Mobley, longtime pastor of Forgiveness Baptist Church, is survived by granddaughter Susan Pratt Chartier, and three great-grandchildren, Steven Chartier, Robert Chartier, and Emily Rose Chartier, all of Northdale, Connecticut; by cousin James Prince, with whom she made her home for many years; and by a host of other relatives and friends.

Mrs. Mobley was preceded in death by her husband in 1981, by son John Henry in 1934, son Charles in 1946, and daughter Emily Mobley Pratt in 1966.

Mrs. Mobley has been a lifelong member of Forgiveness Baptist Church. The wake will be held at Prince Funeral Home and Chapel, from 7:00 to 8:00 P.M. Thursday. Services will be at 11:00 A.M. Friday at the church with the Reverend Carlton Hilton officiating. Burial will follow at Live Oak Cemetery.

Memorial contributions may be made to the Ragsdale House Restoration Fund, in care of Marcus Overton, chairman.

ABOUT THE AUTHOR

IN FEBRUARY 1991, Carolyn Meyer attended the dedication ceremony of a historic marker in the city park a few blocks from her home in Denton, Texas. The bronze plaque explained how the park had been the home of a thriving African American community, called Quakertown (reportedly named after the abolitionist Pennsylvania Quakers), until 1923, when the black residents were required to move to make room for the park.

Curious about the circumstances that resulted in the uprooting of this community, Ms. Meyer set out to uncover the historical facts. The result of her research was the critically acclaimed and popular novel *White Lilacs*.

Ms. Meyer has always been interested in how conflicts of race and culture affect people's lives. She has written numerous books that explore racial differences and similarities, including those listed below.

Gideon's People: When a freak wagon accident occurs, an Amish farm boy and a Jewish peddler's son discover that despite their different upbringings they really are similar—especially when it comes to questioning the values they have been taught.

Drummers of Jericho: Culturally sophisticated fourteen-year-old Pazit moves to her father's home in a small suburban town in Texas and quickly realizes that kids in this high school don't take kindly to outsiders—especially not to Jewish girls with strange names.

Rio Grande Stories: Seventh graders celebrate the diverse cultural heritages and heroes—from low riders and *curanderas* to Navajo code talkers—that make up the rich history and culture of their New Mexican community.

Where the Broken Heart Still Beats: The kidnapping of Cynthia Ann Parker by Comanche Indians is horrifying and frightening; but her return to the white community twenty-four years later is even more painful.

If you'd like to receive more information about Carolyn Meyer, to find out how to order her books, or to write to her, please write to:

Harcourt Brace & Company
Children's Book Division/Marketing Department
525 B Street, Suite 1900
San Diego, CA 92101-4403